ALL IS SI

Manuel Rivas was born in Coruña in 1957. He writes in the Galician language of north-west Spain. He is well known in Spain for his journalism, as well as for his prize-winning short stories and novels, which include the internationally acclaimed *The Carpenter's Pencil* and *Books Burn Badly*. His works have been translated into twenty languages.

Jonathan Dunne translates from Bulgarian, Catalan, Galician and Spanish. He has translated six books by Manuel Rivas into English. He is the editor and translator of the two-volume *Anthology of Galician Literature 1196-1981/1981-2011* and of the *Poetry Review* supplement *Contemporary Galician Poets*. His recent translations include *At the End of the World: Contemporary Poetry from Bulgaria*.

ALSO BY MANUEL RIVAS

Fiction

The Carpenter's Pencil
Butterfly's Tongue
Vermeer's Milkmaid
In the Wilderness
Books Burn Badly

Poetry

From Unknown to Unknown
The Disappearance of Snow

MANUEL RIVAS

All Is Silence

TRANSLATED FROM THE GALICIAN BY
Jonathan Dunne

VINTAGE BOOKS
London

Published by Vintage 2014

2 4 6 8 10 9 7 5 3 1

First published with the title *Todo é silencio* in 2010 by
Edicións Xerais de Galicia

First published in Great Britain in 2013 by
Harvill Secker

Vintage
Random House, 20 Vauxhall Bridge Road,
London SW1V 2SA

www.vintage-books.co.uk

Addresses for companies within The Random House Group Limited
can be found at: www.randomhouse.co.uk/offices.htm

The Random House Group Limited Reg. No. 954009

A CIP catalogue record for this book is available from the British Library

ISBN 9780099565390

This book has been selected to receive financial assistance from
English PEN's 'PEN Translates!' programme, supported by Arts
Council England. English PEN exists to promote literature and our
understanding of it, to uphold writers' freedoms around the world,
to campaign against the persecution and imprisonment of writers
for stating their views, and to promote the friendly cooperation of
writers and the free exchange of ideas. www.englishpen.org.

The Random House Group Limited supports the Forest Stewardship
Council® (FSC®), the leading international forest-certification
organisation. Our books carrying the FSC label are printed on FSC®-
certified paper. FSC is the only forest-certification scheme supported
by the leading environmental organisations, including Greenpeace.
Our paper procurement policy can be found at:
www.randomhouse.co.uk/environment

Printed and bound in Great Britain by Clays Ltd, St Ives Plc

All Is Silence

I   Friendly Silence

1

'The mouth is not for talking. It's for keeping quiet.'

This was one of Mariscal's sayings, which his father repeated like a litany and Víctor Rumbo – Brinco – recalled when the other boy saw with amazement what was in the strange package he'd pulled out of the basket and asked what he wasn't supposed to.

'What's that then? What are you going to do?'

'They have mouths, and speak not,' replied Brinco laconically.

The tide was out, or thinking of coming in, the calm of the waters shocked and shining, which seemed somehow strange. There were the two of them, Brinco and Fins, near the breakwater formed by the rocks, next to the lighthouse on Cape Cons, and not far from the stone crosses that commemorate lost sailors.

In the sky, the beam from the lighthouse acting as epicentre, the seagulls pecked at the silence. There was a mocking wisdom in the way these birds kept watch. An alert grumbling. They moved off in order to come closer, drawing circles that were ever more insolent. They took this liberty, sharing with abandon a secret the rest of existence chose to ignore. Brinco glanced over at them, amused by their scandal. He knew he was the cause of their excitement. They were waiting for something. A definitive sign.

'My dad knows the names of all these rocks,' said Fins in an attempt to detach himself from the course of events. 'The ones you can see and those you can't.'

Brinco had learned by now how to show contempt. He loved the taste of sentences that stung the palate.

'Rocks are just a bunch of old rocks.'

He grabbed the stick of dynamite, which was already fitted with a fuse. As if he knew what he was doing.

'Your dad may be a good sailor, that I do not deny. But now you're going to see some real fishing.'

He finally set light to the fuse. Showed enough composure to hold the stick of dynamite in the air, in front of Fins' face. And then chucked it skilfully over the top of the stone crosses. After a while they heard it explode in the sea.

They waited. The gulls grew more excited, a pack on the wing, egging Brinco on with their screams, celebrating each leap he made on the rocks. Fins kept his eyes firmly on the sea.

'This will be a mark of fear now.'

'You what?'

'The fish won't come back. Wherever someone sets off dynamite, they refuse to return.'

'Why? Because your dad says so?'

'Everybody knows that. It's because of all the mess.'

'Right,' said Brinco mockingly.

In the Ultramar he'd heard similar things and knew how best to respond. 'I suppose you're going to say now that fish have memory.'

He smiled suddenly. One force overcame another inside him and it was this that articulated the smile. What came into his mouth was another saying of Mariscal's. Guaranteed to produce a victory with Fins Malpica looking increasingly on the back foot, pale and subdued as a penitent. The son of the bearer of the cross.

'If you stay poor for long,' said Brinco with measured emphasis, 'you end up shitting white like a seagull.'

He knew that each of Mariscal's sayings would sweep the board. Never failed. Though it bothered him having such a source of inspiration. There's something funny about Mariscal and his maxims. Even if he closed his ears, they'd still lodge inside him. What gives a cherry its stalk? That's another of his. Another one that lodged inside him. Never fails.

Brinco and Fins sat down on a rock and stuck their bare feet in a tidal pool. In this aquarium the only life on view was the animal garden of anemones. They played at drawing their toes closer, a movement which made the false flowers shake their tentacles.

'Bastards,' said Brinco. 'They look like flowers, but they're really leeches.'

'Their mouth is also their bottom,' said Fins. 'It's the same hole, their mouth and bottom.'

The other boy stared at him in amazement. Was about to proffer some rebuke. But thought better of it and remained quiet. Fins Malpica knew much more than he did about fish and animals. And all the rest. At least in school. So Brinco decided to catch something in the pool and stuff it inside his mouth. He closed his mouth and kept his face swollen like a lung. Then he opened it and produced a tiny, live crab on his tongue.

'How long can you hold your breath?'

'I don't know. About half an hour or so.'

Fins became thoughtful. Smiled inside. This was the game with Brinco, you had to let yourself lose in order to keep him happy. Pretend you were a fool.

'Half an hour?' said Fins. 'That's not much.'

It was the first time they'd laughed together since reaching Cape Cons. Brinco stood up and gazed out to sea. With this movement, shielding his eyes with his hand, the din in the sky grew louder. The fierce screams pierced the atmosphere at its weakest point. The first dead fish turned up in the foam, as if parboiled by the sea. Brinco goes after them with his net. Their intestines are all over the place. In the attritional palm of his hand, the contrast between the silver gleam of their skin and the blood of their gills is greater.

'You see? Now is that, or is that not, a miracle?'

2

He was the son of Jesus Christ. The son of Lucho Malpica. People would say, 'That's Lucho's son' or, identifying him with his mother, 'That's Amparo's son.' But he was better known because of his father. Among other things, his father had spent the last few years playing Christ on the day of the Passion, Good Friday. When he was younger, he'd taken the part of a Roman soldier. He'd even held the whip with which to lash the back of Edmundo Sirgal, the Christ before him, who'd also been a sailor. But Edmundo had left for the oil rigs in the North Sea. The first year he'd managed to return in order to be crucified. But then there'd been some problem. People leave and sometimes you lose touch. What was needed was a new Christ, and Lucho Malpica was the obvious choice. There was another bearded gentleman who could have done it, Moimenta, but he had one Michelin too many. As the priest pointed out, 'Christ, Christ can be anyone, but he shouldn't be fat. A good Christ isn't fat, he's all fibre.' And there was Lucho Malpica, strong and thin as a rake. Of the same constitution as the wooden cross on his shoulder.

'The Companion? He's half pagan, Don Marcelo,' said a bore from the confraternity.

'Like them all. But the way he plays Christ is first class! Straight out of Zurbarán!'

Malpica didn't stay still. Burned with speed. Brave as well, his guts in the palm of his hand. His son, Félix – Fins to us – was more like his mother. A bit nostalgic. He had his days, of course. We all have our spring tides and neap tides. He had those days when he turned into a zombie, fell quiet. Absorbed in silence.

The point is he was respectful towards his father, but had his confidence. He never asked for his father or Dad. He asked for Lucho Malpica. Outside the house, this sailor was a kind of third man, something separate from son and father. The boy was forced to protect him. Look out for him. Whenever he saw him coming home drunk, he'd run to the door and help him upstairs, put him to bed like a stowaway, so there wouldn't be trouble at home; his mother had no time for these minor shipwrecks. Once, on the road to Calvary, his mother had said, 'Don't call him Lucho when he's carrying the cross.' For Fins, as a boy, it'd been an honour to watch his father being crucified with the crown of thorns, the smear of blood on his forehead, that blond beard, tunic with the golden belt, sandals. His attention was drawn especially to the sandals, since this wasn't a type of footwear worn by men in Noitía. There were women who wore them in summer. One holidaymaker in particular who stayed with her husband at the Ultramar. And painted her toenails. Nails that shone with oyster enamel. Nickel-plated nails. All the boys round-about, pretending to scrabble on the ground for coins. All because of the woman from Madrid with the painted toenails.

Christ's toes had tufts of hair, nails like limpets, and, despite the sandals, doubled over to cling to the ground as when walking on the surface of rocks. Before the procession he called Fins to one side: 'Pop over to the Ultramar and tell Rumbo to give you a bottle of holy water.' He already knew this wasn't water from the stoup. No, he didn't say anything to his mother. No need to worry her. He'd done the job of Cana before. So he applied grease to his shins and ran as fast as he could. On the way back, he decided to take a sip. Just a moistener. To see what it tasted like. If they all swore by it, there must be something about it. And he could do with a pick-up on a day like this. He felt his entrails, and the reverse of his eyeballs, ignite. He breathed in deeply. As the fresh air doused that inner fire, he corked the bottle, wrapped it in the brown paper and pleaded with his feet to arrive in time before his father had lifted the cross.

Back at the procession, he shouted with delight, 'Dad, Dad!'

And his mother murmured, 'Don't call him that, not when he's holding the cross.'

How well he did it, what conviction he put into his performance.

'What a Christ, so verisimilar!' he heard Exile remark to Dr Fonseca. In Noitía, everyone had a second name. Not exactly a nickname. Like having two faces, two identities. Or three. Because Exile was also Lame. And both were the schoolteacher, Basilio Barbeito.

How well he did it, Lucho Malpica. His face contorted with pain, but also dignified, with 'historic distance' as Exile would say, the look of one who knows that the flatterers of yesterday will be the deniers of tomorrow. He even stumbled during the procession.

The weight he carried was great. Some of the lashes, owing to the theatrical enthusiasm of his tormentors, ended up really hurting. And then, along the way, that canticle of women: 'Forgive your people, Lord! Forgive your people, forgive, Lord! Do not be eternally angry.' Exile pointed out that the celestial scenography helped. There was always a passing storm cloud on hand to eclipse the sun.

'Verisimilar. All they need now is to actually kill him.'

'What a horrendous song!' complained Dr Fonseca. 'A people

on its knees, sick with guilt, pleading with God for a smile. A crumb of happiness.'

'Yes, but don't believe it. There's always a touch of irony in what the people do,' remarked Exile. 'Notice it's only the women who are singing.'

Ecce Homo glanced over at his son and winked his left eye. This image would remain engraved on the boy's memory. Together with the teacher's admiring comment. So verisimilar! He sensed what it could mean, but not entirely. It had something to do with the truth, but was somehow superior to the truth. One notch above it. He kept a hold of this word so he could use it to define what most surprised him, amazed him, filled him with desire. Having finally embraced Leda, having finally been able to take that step, leave the islands and advance towards her, that body from the Tenebrous Sea, what he thought was it couldn't possibly be true. It was all so barbarous, so free, so verisimilar.

3

With the swaying of the coffin, in that dark, enclosed space, Fins found it difficult to breathe.

The space was a real coffin floating on the sea, not far from the shore where the waves break and foam. Like a barge, it was tethered by a rope which Brinco held on to. He pulled on the rope, bringing the coffin closer and then letting it go with the ebb and flow of the waters. Next to him, on the sand, were caskets, some broken, some intact, strange moribund containers, their red lining on view, perplexed remains of a shipwreck in the beyond.

This game began to unsettle him. To calm down, as he did whenever he felt himself suffocating, Fins timed his agitated breathing to the sound and rhythm of the beating waves.

He counted ten inhalations. And shouted, 'Brinco, Brinco! Get me out of here, you bastard!'

He waited. He didn't hear a voice or notice any special movement that might indicate his call was being heeded. Sometimes he'd talk to himself. He thought this was another peculiarity of his, a further derivation of the *petit mal*. But when one discovers a fault, one normally tries to find out to what extent that fault is commonplace. And he'd come to the conclusion that everybody spoke to themselves. His mother. His father. The fishwives. The gatherers of shellfish and seaweed. The washerwomen. The milk-maid. The navvy. Blind Birimbau. The priest. Exile. Dr Fonseca on his solitary walks. The man in charge of the Ultramar, Brinco's dad, whenever he was polishing the glasses. Mariscal after knocking the ice cubes together in his glass of whisky. Leda with bare feet on the frill of the waves. Everybody seemed to do it.

'What a bastard. I'm going to tear your soul from your body. All the worms off your head.'

He deliberately banged his forehead against the coffin lid. Started shouting again, at the limit of his strength by now. An international cry for help. 'Víctor, you son of a bitch!'

He reconsidered. There was another possibility. One that made him really mad, 'I curse the father who made you, Brinco!'

Well, if that didn't arouse an immediate response, he would have to give up. He took a deep breath. Dreamed that Nine Moons had come to lend him a hand. And along the seashore, barefoot, playing at walking the high wire with her flip-flops in her hand, Leda arrived. She was balancing a basket on her head, crammed full of sea urchins.

When he saw the girl, Brinco tugged the coffin towards the shore.

'What are you doing? That brings bad luck.'

Brinco brought his forefinger to his mouth to make her be quiet. Leda deposited her basket on the sand and hurried over to see the remains of futuristic death scattered all over the beach.

'Stop messing around and help!' said the boy.

Leda paid attention and helped to pull on the rope until the floating coffin was back on firm ground.

'Inside is a disgusting insect,' mocked Brinco. 'Come and see!'

Leda peered over with curiosity, but also with distrust.

Brinco lifted the lid of the box. Fins remained motionless,

pale-faced, holding his breath, his arms tied to his body with a tightly fastened belt, eyes closed, in the posture of the deceased.

Leda stared at him in amazement, unable to speak.

'Are you getting up or not, Calamity?' mocked Brinco. 'Our Lady of the Sea is here to see you.'

Fins opened his eyes. And met Leda's astonished expression. She kneeled down and stared at him with eyes wide open, glistening slightly, but also suddenly filled with joy. What she came out with was a protest, 'You're a couple of idiots. Death is hardly a game.'

Leda touched Fins' eyelids with her fingertips.

'A game? He was dead,' said Brinco. 'You should have seen him. He went all pale and stiff . . . Blimey, Fins! You looked just like a corpse.'

Leda watched Fins, sounding him with her eyes, as if she wanted to share a secret with his body. 'It's nothing. They're just absences.'

'Absences?'

'Yes, absences, that's what they're called. Absences. It's nothing. And don't go blabbering about it!'

The girl looked up and soon changed her tone. 'And these coffins?'

'They have an owner already.'

'That wouldn't be your dad by any chance?'

'What's wrong with that? He saw them first.'

'Funny, isn't it?' exclaimed Leda ironically. 'He's always the first.'

Brinco's expression turned sour. 'You have to be awake when others are sleeping.'

Leda glared at him, still mocking, 'Of course you do. That's why they say your dad goes around howling at night.'

He'd have liked to fight her. They'd done this once, played at fighting. The three of them. Whenever he sees her, he starts to feel difficulty breathing. Fury rising in his body. The thumping of his heart injecting a burning red neon light into his eyes. She's prettier when she's silent. She doesn't know that the mouth is for keeping quiet.

'You better be careful what things you howl, Nine Moons.'

'One day someone will tear your soul from your body,' she replied. Whenever she got mad, she spoke differently. In a voice with shadow.

'You've plenty of tongue, but you don't scare me.'

'They'll pluck the worms from your head one by one.'

Fins rose from the coffin, suddenly wide awake, and quickly made to change the subject. 'So is it true you're going to sell these coffins at the inn?'

'We sell lots there,' said Brinco. 'Anyway, you shut up, you're dead.'

4

The main beach in Noitía was shaped like a half-moon. To the south lay the fishing district of San Telmo, which had grown as a shoot of the village which started it all, A de Meus, with its stone houses and sea-painted doors and windows. Further south were the disused salting places and the last drying place of octopus and eel. There, sheltered from the widows' wind, the ramp of the first harbour was preserved. After the rocks of Balea Point came Corveiro Bay. In the middle of it all, the town, spilling new buildings like scattered dominoes. Between San Telmo and Noitía, following the coastal road and before reaching the bridge at Lavandeira da Noite, was Chafariz Cross. From there started a smaller road which climbed uphill to the Ultramar inn, bar, shop, cellar, with its adjoining dance hall and cinema Paris-Noitía.

The far north, where the river Mor and its reed bed formed a natural border, was still untouched. This was a zone of dunes, the oldest with abundant vegetation to leeward, with a predominance of the bluey-green patience of sea holly. The front line of dunes was very steep, where the vanguard of the storm hit first. At the top of these dunes, tied down with the long hair of Bermuda grass, rose a crest of marram grass against the wind.

Further north, protected by a natural armour of rocks, was another, more isolated beach. But anyone looking for it, after a pine grove to the rear of dead dunes, would find the emblazoned gate and walls of Romance Manor.

Which is why the vans stopped before that, at one end of the half-moon, where there were barely any bathers even in summer, except on a public holiday. Most holidaymakers didn't make it past the reeds. But people in vans were not holiday-makers. They were something else. Some arrived at other times of the year. Like these two, this couple, who'd left their van in a corner at the end of the track used as a car park, at the start of the dunes. It was a Volkswagen which had been fitted out as a caravan and painted the colours of the rainbow, with curtains on the windows.

Leda didn't say a word. She was used to doing things like this, of her own free will and on the quiet. What Fins and Brinco did was follow her. They clambered up the inside of a dune until they were confronted by the sea. Hidden by the crest of marram grass, they could see without being seen. There they were, the couple. Rather than swimming, they played at moving away and coming closer with their bodies. In the waves, in foamy whirlpools, attempting not to lose their footing. In the end, both man and woman emerged from the sea. They were holding hands and ran laughing over the sand in the direction of the dunes. They were both tall and slim. She had long, blond hair. It was a luminous day with a young, springy kind of light which glistened on the sea. To the spies, what they were seeing resembled a hypnotic mirage.

'They're hippies,' said Brinco with a certain contempt. 'I heard about them in the Ultramar.'

And Leda murmured, 'Well, they look Dutch or something to me.'

'Sssssssh!'

Amid laughter, Fins told them to be quiet. The couple, seeking somewhere to hide, came closer to the peeping Toms. The lovers caressed each other with their bodies, but also with the ebb and flow of their breath, their words.

'Ohouijet'aimejet'aimeaussibeaucouptuestplusbellequele-soleil tu m'embrasses.'

'Ohouioucefeudetapeautuvienstuvienstumetues tu me fais du bien.'

The accelerated pleasure of bodies on sand, that pleasurable violence, the throbbing of their whispers, unsettled the sentinels. Fins ducked down and leaned against the inner slope of the dune, and the other two copied him.

'That was French,' said the red-faced Fins in a whisper.

'Who cares?' said Brinco. 'You can understand everything.'

It was Leda who decided to take one last look. And what she saw was the torso of the woman on top of the man, astride him, copulating, lifting her head to the sky and stopping all the wind, tensing her body, filling the horizon, everything an attentive gaze could take in. At the highest point, the woman closed her eyes, and so did Leda.

Then Leda started rolling downhill. And Fins and Brinco had no choice but to follow her.

'If they're hippies, I suppose they'd be talking hippy.'

They'd already passed the bridge by the reeds, but were still a little nervous. Their bodies had yet to settle in their bodies. From time to time a mouth would let out a blast. They didn't talk about what they'd seen, but what they'd heard.

The other two burst out laughing. Leda didn't like it.

'I was only joking!'

'No you weren't,' said Brinco in order to wind her up. And he continued the joke: 'Hippies speak hippy!'

'You're a couple of idiots. You've a screw loose.'

'Don't get mad,' said Fins. 'Nothing's wrong.'

'You can go to hell, go write on water,' shouted Leda. 'You're both the same.'

5

They walked, deep in thought, along the side of the coastal road. The two boys had their hands in their pockets and were watching Leda's bare feet on the tarmac. She played with her flip-flops, humming the tune of 'Lola' and swinging them in the air like huge dragonflies.

When they reached Chafariz Cross, on the other side of the road leading to the Ultramar, they saw another boy who was younger than them. He was calling to them and waving his arm urgently.

'It's Chelín! He must have found something,' exclaimed Leda.

Brinco cannot avoid being sarcastic whenever he sees Chelín. 'Sure, he'll have found something. He doesn't know how to live without that damn pendulum.'

'Well, it works sometimes, doesn't it, Leda?' said Fins in a conciliatory tone.

'Only because he's so damn stubborn,' replied Brinco.

Leda gazed at them both as if rebuking them for their ignorance. 'His dad used to unearth springs. He was clairvoyant, a water diviner. He discovered all the wells in this area with a rod or pendulum. There are people like that, who see into what's hidden. With magnetic powers.' She learned her trade in the river and sea, washing and collecting shellfish. Her speech had a gurgle that made her stand out. An excess load that acted as defence. And she still had time to murmur with what was left of her open body. 'Some people are just smoke. They don't kill or frighten, tie or untie.'

'Amen,' replied Brinco.

'That must be why he's so good at stopping the ball,' interjected Fins. 'Hidden powers!'

'Maybe. But where the hell is he taking us?'

Leda ran to meet Chelín. She knew where they were going. For a short while the path became deeper, surrounded on either side by clumps of laurel, holly and elder, which bent down as if to form a vault. It finally gave way to a stone staircase. Next to each step, fermenting moss that resembled a curled-up hedgehog. Suddenly, on top of the hill, a house which seemed to be propped up, supported, by nature. One of those ruins that wants to disappear but can't, which is bound, not cleft, by the ivy on the walls. Behind a tangle of gorse and broom were two hollows. A dislocated wooden door and a distrustful window with a squint. The building was so taken by nature that the visible part of the roof was a field of foxgloves, and at the eaves the thickest branches of ivy intertwined in order to fall back on themselves as gargoyles. On the threshold of the door, the leaves had respected the tiles, perhaps because of their vegetal forms, which were modernist in style, orange and green, and adorned an inscription in letters glazed blue on white: 'American Union of Sons of Noitía, 1920'.

Chelín was taken up with his role. He concentrated all his senses, outside and in, just as his clairvoyant father had taught him. There was something special about the pendulum in his hand. The magnetic weight at the end of the chain was a bullet.

To start with, it didn't move. But then slowly the pendulum began to sway from side to side.

Leda rebuked the disbelievers: 'See?'

'He's doing it with his wrist,' replied Brinco. 'You're a fraud, Chelín. Here, give it to me.'

Chelín ignored him. Because he knew Brinco was a stick-in-the-mud, and because he really was following another clue. Absorbed in the intricacy of flows, deposits and currents. He started walking towards the hollow of the door, the pendulum swaying ever more quickly.

'Come on, have no fear!' exclaimed Leda with conviction, because she knew Brinco was more than reluctant. Normally so forward, he always came up with excuses here, warned that the place was dangerous, on the verge of collapsing.

The inside of the School of Indians was largely in shadow, but there was a crater in the roof through which entered a substantial beam of light. A natural skylight opened by a circular cascade of tiles. And there were other, smaller holes, cracks through which entered spears or arrows with the nature of sun rays. The air was so thick that the light found it difficult to penetrate as far as the ground. But it was important it did so, both for the intruders and for the place itself. Because what this beam of light and the occasional slender lantern illuminated was the large relief map of the world which covered the floor. Carved in noble wood, it had been treated, varnished, skilfully painted and preserved, not with the idea of eternity, but so that it could accompany as optimistic ground, somewhere between time and the intemporal, the future of Noitía. In the American Union of Sons of Noitía's school, built with the donations of emigrants, there was this peculiarity, which was later copied: each pupil sat in a corner of the *mappa mundi* and moved with the passing of the years, so that when he finished, he could be said to be a citizen of the world. There were other things that made the so-called School of Indians unusual. The typewriters and sewing machines sent from Argentina or Uruguay. The impressive library, imported or paid for. The zoological collection with the presence of desiccated animals and birds in glass cases, according to the custom of that period. There was still the odd specimen, the spectre of some bird which had been left for an unknown reason, like the long-necked crane hanging incredulous next to the detachable pedagogical skeleton missing an arm. On the main wall, faded like cave paintings, the trees of Natural Sciences and the History of Civilisations. Faded as was the map on the ground, over which the children walked, with Chelín and his pendulum leading the way, across countries and continents, islands and seas, the geographical names still discernible, despite the gnawing and abandonment of time.

Chelín came to a halt. The pendulum was swinging like crazy. He'd brought them to a shady corner where they could make out a bulky shape covered in a brand-new tarpaulin, which upped their expectations, since the visitors weren't much interested in relics. A large part of the furniture and collections had burned in another time, an archaic period outside time, referred to by the grown-ups as 'war'. There were still a few books on the dusty shelves, subsumed by cobwebs and rilled by lice. Not much was left. A few furtive visitors would come and rummage through the rotten, gnawed, fearful remains. Though each year the population of bats increased, hanging on their shadowy hooks.

Nobody dared. In the end, Chelín took hold of the bullet and decided to lift one end of the tarpaulin. They were silenced, astonished.

'Well done, Chelín! Now that's what I call a treasure.'

It was a large cargo of boxes full of bottles of whisky. The discoverers of the haul gazed in fascination at the image of the tireless Johnnie Walker.

Leda moved forward and managed to extract a bottle with the famous label of the rare and much sought-after imported whisky. She turned to Chelín and declared a historical redress in admiring tones: 'You're our hero, Chelín!'

Fins pointed at him triumphantly. 'No more Chelín. From now on, Johnnie. Johnnie Walker! Our captain!'

The blast of a shotgun echoed around the old school's interior as if propelled by the core of this last sentence. The echo. The fragments of tile. The crazed flight of the bats. The bulging eyes of the clairvoyant's son. Everything seemed to have come from the weapon's smoking barrel. Leda was so dazed she dropped the bottle of whisky, which fell to the ground and smashed in a bluey area named 'The Atlantic Ocean'.

Two figures emerged from the darkness with absolutely no intention of passing unnoticed, and came to a halt beneath the accidental skylight in the roof. The first to make himself visible was a giant hulk carrying the shotgun. But he was soon replaced in the foreground by a second man wearing a white suit and panama hat, who wiped away his sweat with a crimson handkerchief without removing his white cotton gloves.

They knew who it was. They knew it was useless trying to escape.

He took possession. The large bully dusted off a chair and offered it to his superior. When he started talking, he did so in a deep voice, which was both intimate and imperative. The man was Mariscal, 'the Authentic', as he himself liked to be known. The other man, the one with the weapon, was Carburo, his inseparable bodyguard. Nobody used that word. He was the Curate. The Stick under Orders. The Bully. This was his name. He'd worked for a time as a butcher, and used this snippet from his CV whenever he thought it appropriate, with convincing self-esteem.

'I shit on the keys of life, Carburo! Don't worry, boys, don't worry . . . This oaf has a taste for artillery. I'm always telling him, "Carburo, ask first. Then do what you have to." *A fortiori*. These things happen. You finger the trigger, it's the trigger that's in charge. As the philosopher once said, with gunpowder and a kick in the balls, that was the end of man.'

Mariscal became thoughtful, his gaze fixed on the ground. The wood-carved map in relief. The work that must have gone into it, the work involved in remembering.

He raised his eyes and noticed Leda. 'Where did this girl come from?'

'I came from the mother who had me!' exclaimed Leda in a rage. She was furious about the loss.

'*Kyrie eleison*,' said Mariscal after a pause. 'And who is that saint, if one may ask?'

'Not "is"', said Leda. 'She died when I was born.'

Mariscal clicked his tongue and leaned over. He seemed now to be inspecting the trail of lights in the ceiling. You grew up well, girl, he murmured to himself. Nature is wise. Very wise. History returns, he thought, and it's good to step aside. He recalled Adela, an employee at the canning factory where Guadalupe used to work. He didn't stop still until he'd bought the factory. He hated the owner, the foreman, those stingy, sticky exploiters. Let them go grope their own mothers. The owner didn't want to sell, but had no choice in the matter. And when the factory was his, he said to Guadalupe, 'Now they can sing and eat all they like.' But that was only for a while. He ended up employing the same foreman. Adela? Yes, Adela. Her beauty, her shyness, her resistance, her sudden yielding, her unfathomable sadness in the mezzanine after what happened happened. She shut herself up at home. Never came back to work. Somebody convinced Antonio Hortas, a poor, single sailor, to marry her and give his surname to the baby. Antonio didn't need much convincing. Or paying. Because Antonio Hortas loved that woman. And if it was a question of horns, he didn't mind; he knew plenty of illustrious members of the Confraternity of St Cornelius.

God keeps an eye on the devil, who's just a poor old demon. God gives as much as he has to give.

'*Mutatis mutandis*,' murmured Mariscal, avoiding the girl's gaze. And then recovering his tone of voice, 'Well, troops . . . there's an end to it. You heard nothing. You saw nothing. *Os habent, et non loquentur.* They have mouths, and speak not. Learn that and you've gained half a life. The rest is also very simple. *Oculos habent, et non videbunt.* They have eyes, and see not. *Aures habent, et non audient.* They have ears, and hear not.'

In the ruinous School of Indians, his voice sounded charming, velvety and hoarse. They were all ears and eyes.

He fell silent. Sized up the weight of his charm. Then added, '*Manus habent, et non palpabunt.* They have hands, and touch not. Don't pay much attention to that. The hands are for touching and the feet are for walking. But it fits the bill when things have an owner. As is the case here.'

They listened like schoolchildren being treated to an impromptu masterclass. Here was a man acting himself and revelling in the role. He cleared his throat. Stroked his lips.

'It's very important to know why the senses exist. What are the eyes for? For not seeing. There's what cannot be seen, cannot be heard, cannot be said. And, in this last case, what cannot be said you have to suppress and keep your trap shut. What about the mouth? The mouth is for keeping quiet. That's the funny thing about Latin, one thing leads to another.'

Brinco understood perfectly the meaning of Mariscal's words. But what he liked best was the way he said them. That assuredness. That manner of asserting control with a hint of scorn, which captivated and drew you in with an obscure sense of sympathy. He felt linked to him by an invisible intelligence.

A force stronger than that of rebellion, but which couldn't override it completely. Shit. His guts. The way they rumble so it seems everyone can hear. That whiny bastard, how Mariscal likes to talk. To listen to himself. The mouth is for keeping quiet.

Víctor Rumbo made as if to leave. Started to do so.

'Brinco, stay where you are. I haven't finished yet.'

Mariscal approached the teacher's desk, mounted the platform and, possibly because of his position, raised his voice, giving free rein to his discourse. 'You have to differentiate between reality and dreams. That's the firstest thing.' He laughed at his grammatical error. 'The first is always the firstest.' Then he recovered his grand gesture, his sobriety. 'The day you get that confused, you're lost. So walk very carefully, children. There are bad people about, people who on account of a Johnnie Walker, one miserable smuggled bottle, will hang you from a butcher's hook.'

Mariscal turned his gaze towards the wall with the faded Tree of History.

'History started with a crime,' he said abruptly. 'Haven't they taught you that yet?'

He interrupted himself. Seemed to gauge the weight of his own words. Stared at the map on the floor and murmured tiredly, 'Enough lessons for today!'

The glare of lightning illuminated the ocean inside the School of Indians. They waited, but the clap of thunder held back, as if summoning all its strength to burst through the crater in the roof intact.

'Home, all of you! The beams of heaven are about to cave in!'

6

Lucho Malpica was shaving in front of a small mirror with a diagonal crack, which hung next to the window opposite the sea. Half his face was covered in shaving foam, which he removed with the razor, leaving half Christ's beard. From time to time he would stop and stare sombrely through the window, in search of signs in the sea and sky.

'Seems like the old so-and-so has finally calmed down.'

Into a cushion used for knitting lace, on top of the stencilled pattern, a woman's hands, Amparo's, stuck pins with different-coloured heads which appeared to be inventing a map of their own. The hands paused for a moment. They also were on the lookout for Malpica's embittered voice.

'How long is it since I last went fishing, Amparo?'

'Some time.'

'How long?'

'A month and three days.'

'Four. A month and four days.'

Then he added a piece of information he immediately regretted. But he'd said it already. 'Do you know where there's a tally? In the Ultramar's book of IOUs. That's where they keep track of the stormy weather. Some sailors never leave that place.'

'They shouldn't have gone there to start with,' said Amparo angrily. 'Let them drown their sorrows at home.'

'You have to do something. God knows, I wish I were in prison!'

Amparo raised her eyes and responded with irony, 'And me in hospital!'

Seated at the table, Fins watched these two words, 'prison' and 'hospital', cross the tablecloth and build a strange abode in the red and white squares of the oilskin. A space that was quickly occupied by the creatures from the book he was reading, which twisted and turned and which until now had been unknown to him.

Amparo's hands took up their work. They moved with the urgency of arriving somewhere as soon as possible. As they managed the boxwood needles, the sound of the wood formed a musical percussion which seemed both to mark and to follow the rhythm of the man's restless pacing, of the storm in his head.

'So me in prison and you in hospital. What fun! This life is for letting off fireworks!'

Her hands dropped to her lap. 'You're getting worse, Lucho. You used to have more patience. And more humour.'

The sailor pretended to zip up his mouth. Felt guilty for the sense of unease. Attempted a smile. 'I used to cry with one eye and laugh with the other.'

Fins had been dividing his imagination and gaze between the print of his parents and the illustration in his book. He took advantage of his father's sudden silence. 'Dad, have you ever seen an Argonaut?'

The sailor sat down at the table, next to his son. Thought about it. 'Well, there was a Russian boat that went down once. The sailors wore heavy leather jackets. Black leather jackets. Good they were too . . .'

'No, Dad. I'm not talking about people. Have a read of this: "Such cephalopods are very ugly animals. If one looks inside an Argonaut's eyes, one sees that they are empty."'

Fins looked up from the book and stared at his father. Lucho's expression was one of enormous surprise. He was running through all the sea creatures he knew. He thought about the rainbow wrasse, which some years was male and others female. He thought . . . But no, he'd never gazed into an Argonaut's empty eyes.

'That book came from the School of Indians,' he said. He poured himself a glass of claret and emptied it in one go.

'Why was it called that? School of Indians?'

Lucho's hurt gesture. His smile. He always made the most of this opportunity. Fins knew what he was going to say, the same old joke about playing cowboys and Indians, being an Apache and so on. But this time a flicker of pain interrupted his smile. A spasm introduced by memory.

'Many from here – many! – left for America. Most were stonemasons, carpenters, bricklayers, day labourers . . . and sailors. Once they'd got themselves a bit of silver, the first thing they'd do is go and buy themselves a suit for dancing. The next thing, get together in order to set up a school. That's what they did. All over Galicia. It was for them the Modern School. But after the war, when it was abandoned, it got this other name, School of Indians.'

He glanced over at Amparo, who was slowly inserting pins into the cushion.

'It wasn't just any old school. It was the best school! Everything they had hoped for. Rationalist, they called it. And they sent typewriters, sewing machines, globes, microscopes, barometers . . . They even packed in a skeleton so we could learn the names of all the bones. They set up loads of schools, but this one had something special. An extraordinary idea that the floor of the school was the world. They made it out of noble wood. That floor was built by the very best carpenters and carvers. Every now and then, you'd sit in a different country.'

He fell silent. Made an inventory. In this composition of the thinker, he held his head with such pressure, so horizontally, that he seemed to be stopping a leak in his temple.

'That's all that's left, more or less. The floor and the skeleton.'

He stood up and with his right forefinger started pointing at his left hand, 'Trapezium, trapezoid, capitate, hamate . . .' One word jumped on top of another. Lucho Malpica was content. He noticed the fizz of memory on his lips, the fact that he could remember. That salty taste.

'Do you know which is the most important bone of all? No, you don't.' He smacked his son on the nape. 'The sphenoid!'

Lucho then made a bowl with his scarred hands and declared, as if holding a human skull, 'I can hear the teacher now. Here's the key, the sphenoid! The bone with a chair like a Turkish bed and a bat's wings, which opened in silence all through history to make room for the enigmatic organisation of the soul.'

He stared at his hands in surprise, the bowl of eloquence they'd made. Then exclaimed in amazement at himself, 'Blessed hosts!'

The other two, mother and son, also stared at him in wonder. He was a taciturn type. On the quiet side. At home there was a connection between his ruminations and the knocking together of the boxwood needles. To Fins, when he became aware of it, this was a wounding sound. A chattering of the house's teeth. But there were these moments, increasingly rare, when the sound became transfigured. And the cud showed itself.

'Which parts of the world did you sit in, father?' asked Fins with shared enthusiasm.

Lucho Malpica suddenly changed tone. 'I don't want you going there.'

'Any day now the sky will fall on top of you!' added his mother.

Lucho went over to the window to take a look at the sea. From there, he spoke to his son in an imperative tone. 'Listen, Fins, you need to go and clean the vats again.'

'He's too big to be getting into those vats,' remarked Amparo angrily. 'Besides, he gets dizzy.'

'Not half as much as at sea,' mumbled Lucho.

He got down on his knees by the hearth in order to stoke the fire. At his back, the smoke imitated the seascape, taking the form of mists and storm clouds. 'What do you want me to do, woman? Rumbo asked me. I can't tell him no.'

'Well, it's about time you learned to say no once in a while!'

Lucho ignored his wife. If only she knew the times he'd had to say no. He decided to speak to his son, and did so vehemently. 'Listen, Fins! Don't go telling anyone about your absences. If you talk about it, you'll never get a job. Understand? Don't ever talk about it. Ever! Not even to the walls.'

Amparo took up her work and the boxwood needles resounded again like the house's anguished inner music. There was now a thread connecting the lacemaker's imagination and the way the needles knocked together. In Amparo's mind, seeing what she'd seen, there were new and old times. On occasion, the new times even gave birth to the old. Which was why she preferred not to let the memories show themselves. The shadowy mouths had had their say. When she was a girl, anyone who suffered from epileptic fits or prolonged absences ended up being considered mad. A simple nickname like that could land you in the madhouse.

A great-aunt had died there. Back when each internee had a

number tattooed on their skin. There had even been professional loony hunters who'd visited remote villages and poor districts in covered wagons like cages, searching for suitable candidates. The Church, in league with some powerful families, had founded a hospital. And the administration took money from the local councils according to the number of internees. The more loonies, the better.

Oh yes. She knew what she was talking about. Which was why she kept quiet. And her fingers ran further away.

7

Fins heard the door knocker and knew who was at the door. Three knocks in succession, followed by another. The knocker was a metal hand. A hand Lucho Malpica had found in Corcubión Estuary. He said it came from the *Liverpool*, which had sunk in 1846. He'd cleaned off the rust and polished it very carefully – like a real hand, he said – until it shone again like metal. According to him, the hand of the knocker was the most valuable object in the house. Whenever he came home drunk from one of his personal shipwrecks, he'd stroke the hand, taking care not to bang it.

The three knocks were repeated, followed by another. His mother also knew who this Morse code belonged to. She stopped her knitting and gazed at the door with distrust.

Fins ran to open it. It was her. Leda Hortas.

He had no chance to ask questions. She pulled at him excitedly. First with her eyes. Then she grabbed hold of his arm. Even she wasn't aware of how strong she could be.

'Come on! Run!'

She let go and started running barefoot towards the beach. Fins didn't have time to close the door. When he heard his mother's voice again, he didn't want to. He knew she'd be sitting down, muttering, 'Nine Moons!'

'Where are we going, Leda? What's up?'

But no, she wouldn't stop. Her legs, dark feet, pale heels, seemed to grow as they ran. They laboured their way up the side of the largest primary dune, between corridors of storm, until they reached the top.

She was beside herself, her eyes wide open. 'Look, Fins!'

'My God! It cannot be!'

'That's nothing.'

The beach near where they were was covered in oranges discarded by the sea. The two youngsters remained motionless. Grafted on to the sand. Feeling the Bermuda grass, being tickled by the spikes of marram. In amazement. Turned to wind.

It was a while before Leda and Fins heard the sound of heavy machinery. They were about to jump down the vertical face of sand. Touch the mirage with their hands.

From the top of the dune they saw the lorry making its way with difficulty along the dirt track. It stopped in the clearing at the end of the road, in an area used for extracting sand. A man and a boy got out of the cabin. They knew them both very well. The elder one was Rumbo, who was in charge of the Ultramar. The younger, Brinco. In the trailer three others, Inverno, Chumbo and Chelín, unloaded some baskets or panniers with which to collect the fruit.

Brinco pretended not to notice them. They realised he was pretending.

That's what he was like, thought Fins. When he was absorbed in his own things, he was absorbed in his own things. He'd get annoyed if you stuck your nose in. Turn invisible. Deaf. Mute. But when he wanted your interest, your attention, there was no way of getting rid of him.

At Rumbo's orders, the group started gathering the oranges the sea had brought in from the listing-over of some ship.

'Take a look, Víctor. The sea is a veritable mine,' said Rumbo. 'It gives out everything. Without a single shovelful of manure! You don't have to fertilise it, like the blasted earth.'

Leda jumped down the vertical face and marched towards the group of harvesters. Fins always had the impression that his feet sank in the sand more than hers. She didn't sink, she seemed to walk on the surface. Especially when she had an objective in mind. A destination.

'These oranges are mine!' she shouted. 'I saw them first!'

Rumbo and his companions stopped working. Stared at her in amazement. Except for Brinco. Brinco turned his back on them. Sometimes, when he got annoyed, he'd say, 'You're always sniffing at other people's farts.' But now he preferred not to see them.

The girl squared up to the boss. 'You know the rules. A shipwreck's remains belong to the one who finds them.'

Rumbo gazed at her with a mixture of amusement and confusion. 'How much is the cargo worth then, girl?'

'A lot!'

Leda took in the possessions on the beach with her hands. There were still oranges emerging from the foam. 'Although I'm not sure yet if I want to sell them.'

Rumbo pulled a coin out of his pocket. 'Here you go. For the trouble of seeing.'

'What the hell is that? That's a piece of shit, Mr Rumbo!' said Leda.

The man held the coin between his thumb and forefinger and twirled it mysteriously in front of Leda. 'Close your eyes.'

Leda did as she was told. Fins wasn't sure what was going on. Rumbo flicked the coin in the air and called to the others, 'Now you'll see!'

Rumbo crouched down. Let his hands slide along Leda's naked legs, from the knees downwards, grabbed her right foot, which was bare, and placed it on top of the coin. All the others were waiting, Brinco as well, who'd returned from the land of the invisible.

Rumbo was absorbed in his experiment and murmured, 'Now you'll see, yes, now you'll see what a woman's skin is like.'

Then, out loud, 'Tell me, girl, heads or tails?'

Leda still hadn't opened her eyes. Without a moment's hesitation, 'Tails!'

She moved her foot and uncovered the coin. It was tails. They could see the imperial eagle. Rumbo had a quick look at the other side, Franco's head, where it said *Caudillo of Spain by the grace of God*.

'She's right. It is tails!'

The group of workers burst out laughing. Rumbo produced a wallet from his back pocket and pulled out a hundred-peseta note with the image of the beautiful Fuensanta painted by Romero de Torres. 'Take this. A darkie! The most popular in the whole of Spain! Lots of people keep these stuffed in their mattresses.'

Then, addressing the others, 'Now you see what a woman's skin is like. Even the skin on her foot! This one was born wise. She'll be rich one day. It's written in the stars.'

Leda placed the back of her thumb on her mouth. Quickly made the sign of the cross. And spat in the direction of the sea.

'Poor I won't be.'

8

To be in the dark and scratch darkness with a broom. The dark's boundary smells acrid. This is his work. To scratch the crust of shadows. He feels drunk and dirty inside. Possessed by a putrid intoxication. But his instinct tells him to climb the slope and exit through what resembles a fleshy mouth, opening and closing for him. He lies face up on the stony ground. Out of breath to start with. Then, in and out of his body, he feels a tingle like never before. As if, for a moment, all the attention of the cosmos is centred on him.

He gets up. Looks at the mouth of hell. The great vat. He's still holding the small broom in his hand. His arms and face are covered in grime spread by his sweat. He's wearing old, patched-up clothes stained by the work of cleaning. He feels better, even attracted by the mouth, by the now succulent memory of the dizzy spell and his escape.

It has been a day of great heat, of burning noon. In the yard of the Ultramar the sun is still strong, but the large gate at the end frames a hazy sea, a depression spreading along the coast. Fins Malpica blinks. Finally comes to completely. And swings towards the mouth of the other huge vat, next to the one he's been cleaning.

'Brinco! Hey, Brinco! Can you hear me? Can you hear me or not? Víctor! Brinco!'

Faced by the other's silence, he decides to get into the dark vat. He pulls at Víctor Rumbo with all his might. Grabs him by the ankles, lifts him in his arms and places him on the ground, taking great care not to knock him against the stones. Víctor is unconscious. Alarmed, unsure how best to proceed, Fins kneels down, searching for a pulse or heartbeat, for signs of life in his eyes. But the other boy's hand is limp, his chest doesn't heave and his irises seem to have disappeared. Fins hesitates, then makes up his mind. Gets ready to apply the mouth-to-mouth. He knows how to do it. He is a fisherman's son and has seen cases of people close to drowning on Noitía's beaches.

With both hands he opens Víctor's mouth as wide as he can. Takes a deep breath, and bends down to apply his mouth to the other's. The unconscious victim pouts his lips with mocking exaggeration in preparation for an amorous kiss.

'Mmmm!'

Fins understands he's being made fun of and stands up in annoyance.

Brinco gets to his feet as well and bursts out laughing. He can't stop himself. His laughter seems to have no end. But then he suddenly stops laughing. This happens when he hears the sound of an engine, turns his gaze and sees a car coming up the hill with treacherous calm.

The car halts in the yard, next to where the others are standing. It's a white Mercedes and out gets Mariscal. Looking elegant, always like some kind of beau, in his white suit and panama hat, his shoes white as well. His hands in white gloves like the ones used at gala ceremonies.

'How are things down in hell, boys?'

Brinco looks at him, shrugs his shoulders, but remains quiet.

'Getting by, sir,' replies Fins.

'I've been in there as well!' says Mariscal, addressing the other boy. 'Mmmm! It's strange, but I always liked that smell.'

Without touching the mouths, taking care not to stain his immaculate suit, he goes over to inspect the vats' vast interiors.

'This is a job that needs doing! It certainly does,' he declares in solemn tones. 'If the vats aren't clean . . . what's the word? . . . un-ble-mished . . . the whole crop goes to waste. On account of the tiniest speck of shit. For that simple reason, the whole lot is wasted. Think about it. Imagine one of those vats is the globe. A single speck of shit could finish off the planet.'

Pondering his own statement, with a look of concern, he stresses his point. 'No joke. It could finish off the planet. *Ipso facto*. Think about it!'

Mariscal puts his hand in his pocket and solemnly chucks a coin through the air in Brinco's direction. Brinco grabs it with a swift gesture, as if his arm has acted by itself and is used to this game. But his mouth refuses to say thank you. As for the eyes, any casual observer would think it better, now and in the future, to steer clear of this person's trajectory. But the man in white doesn't seem surprised or affected by the boy's silent hostility.

'And you, you . . .'

'Fins, sir.'

'Fins?'

'Yes, Malpica's son, sir.'

'Malpica! Lucho Malpica! A fine sailor, your dad. One of the best!'

He fumbles in his pocket and throws another coin at Fins, who catches it in the air. Mariscal takes his leave with a greeting, by caressing the brim of his hat.

'Now you know. Not a speck of shit!'

He walks quickly towards the back door of the Ultramar.

He is muttering something. Talking to himself. The memory,

the name of Malpica, bothers him for some reason. 'A fine sailor, yes sirree. *Sensu stricto*. Stubborn as well. One of the dumbest!'

The boys watch him go. Shortly afterwards, when he's disappeared through the door, they hear his ingratiating tones: 'Sira? Sira, are you there?'

His voice echoes in the yard. Fins glances over at Brinco. His gaze now contains the fuse, dynamite, anemones. Like someone playing with a whip, he brushes his feet with the broom.

'What do you say we search for that speck of shit that's going to finish off the world?'

Brinco doesn't want to play along. All Fins gets back is a ration of sullen eyes. Fins knows how the other boy's face can change. He finds it difficult to say, for example, when it's friendly or not, happy or not. Brinco's mood swings from one state to another, as the sky changes in Noitía. His eyes now are focused on the point where Mariscal has gone in. They scour the front of the house, pierce the stones. Gaze up at the windows on the first floor. In one of which the face of the white-suited gallant appears for a moment behind the curtain. A woman slips past him. It's Sira. The man follows. Both vanish from sight in a flicker of shadows.

9

Brinco went in through the back door and climbed an inner staircase which led to the first-floor landing, where the Ultramar's rooms were. On the staircase was a warm light, of the kind afforded by bare bulbs hanging from the ceiling by twisted wires. Up on the landing, the wind introduced gusts of light which clung to the curtains. On the opposite wall, without windows, were a few typical souvenirs: ceramic plates painted with marine scenes, scallop shells, starfish and coral branches on varnished wood, oil paintings of flowers and leaves on polished planks the sea had cast up on the shore.

With a grimy face and tense expression, Brinco walked down the carpeted landing, not bothering to push aside the curtains. He was heading for the room at the end, known by everyone at the inn simply as 'La Suite'. He stopped in front of the closed door.

For a short while he listened to the sighs and murmurs of the amorous struggle. Coming through a door, the human Morse emitted by pleasure sounds remarkably like the language of pain. Brinco suddenly heard his own name. A voice from afar, which penetrated the curtains' turbulence. His father always called him by his Christian name. He didn't like his nickname.

'Víctor! Where the hell are you? Víctor!'

Rumbo's voice made him even angrier. With the back of his sleeve he dried the tears streaming down his grimy face. Left very carefully. Quickened his pace. Started running, furiously barging into the curtains that, with the sash windows half open, seemed to flutter in time, when in fact each was governed by its own wind in rigorous, stormy succession.

The walls of the Ultramar's bar were covered in posters and stills from Westerns. There was also a poster from a local group dressed up as mariachis with the name 'Noitía's Magicians'. And there were a few well-known faces of singers and film stars, all of them women: Sara Montiel, Lola Flores, Carmen Sevilla, Aurora Bautista, Amália Rodrigues, Gina Lollobrigida and Sophia Loren. In the midst of them all, of a smaller size but in a prominent position, a black and white photograph of Sira Portosalvo with the following dedication: 'To the one I most love and make suffer'.

Fins was seated at a table, eating mussels boiled in their shells, which Rumbo had served him when he'd finished cleaning. As he ate, he seemed to watch and listen to everything that was being said. Over at the counter, Rumbo and a couple from the Civil Guard – Sergeant Montes and a younger guard, Vargas – were talking about cinema.

'There I agree one hundred per cent with the authority,' declared Rumbo, staring at the sergeant. 'There's nobody like John Wayne. Wayne and a horse. That's enough to make a film. No need for a pretty girl or anything.'

This categorical exclusion was followed by a silence Rumbo correctly interpreted as profound disagreement.

'Though if there is a pretty girl, it makes for a perfect trio. Wayne, horse and girl, in that order,' he clarified before redirecting the conversation. 'Even though he had to change his name.'

'What do you mean?' asked the sergeant in confusion. 'Wasn't he called John?'

'No, his name wasn't John. His name was . . . Marion.'

'Ma-ri-on?' repeated the sergeant, barely able to suppress his disappointment. 'You don't say!'

Then, after taking a sip of his drink, the sergeant added, 'Someone else who changed his name was Cassius Clay. Now he's called Muhammad Ali or something.'

'That's different entirely,' muttered Rumbo in a low voice, looking in the other direction.

'They're going to throw him in prison because of his refusal to go to war. The world champ! Those Yankees sure don't hang about with half-measures.'

Rumbo's attention was focused on the front door, where Brinco finally appeared. He'd deliberately gone a longer way to avoid coming down the inner stairs. He had the glazed look of someone whom the sea has deposited directly on the shore.

'Where've you been?' asked Rumbo in annoyance. 'I went to the yard, but you weren't there. You left Fins all on his own, cleaning that shit. This boy wasn't born for work, damn it! Couldn't you get him a job as a guard, my sergeant?'

Sergeant Montes slapped Brinco on the back. 'He has himself a good sponsor, Rumbo. Who wouldn't want him? You were born on your feet, lad.'

After that it was Rumbo who felt uncomfortable, taking refuge in the silence at the other end of the bar and making out he was busy. Later he returned, bringing Víctor a sandwich. 'Here you go. It's got omelette inside, don't you know?' he said sarcastically. 'Made by your mother's own fair hands.'

Vargas the guard had remained on the margins. He'd clearly been deep in thought ever since they started discussing cinema. 'You know the one who drives me crazy . . .'

The sergeant didn't let him finish. 'Listen, Rumbo. If the baddy's a good 'un, the film's a good 'un. Now is that or isn't that so?'

'Yes, that's so,' said Rumbo abruptly, with a fixed stare. He was keeping his thoughts to himself.

'For example, I reckon I'd make a real good baddy,' said Sergeant Montes. 'Don't you reckon, Rumbo?'

'I reckon you would, sergeant. A real good baddy.'

The sergeant fell silent, chewing over Rumbo's answer. 'Don't be so sure,' he said finally, with an inquisitive look.

Vargas seemed blissfully unaware that he'd just been party to a short duel of words. He was still trying to finish his sentence. 'As for Westerns, the one who drives me crazy is that woman . . . in *Johnny Guitar* . . . wearing trousers.'

This invocation changed everything. Rumbo grew enthusiastic, as if he could see the screen. 'Vienna, Vienna . . . That's it, Joan Crawford!' he exclaimed, pointing to the guard. 'Clever man. The force is going up in the world, sergeant!'

'But let's be serious,' replied Sergeant Montes. 'For a woman in arms, take *Duel in the Sun*. Can you name her, Rumbo?'

'Jennifer Jones!'

Quique Rumbo, barman at the Ultramar, in charge of the dance hall and cinema Paris-Noitía, was a man of resources. He was seldom prone to exaggeration, but possessed a fine sense of spectacle. He lifted his arms in a liturgical gesture which he prolonged by drawing voluptuous curves in the air.

'*Pange, lingua, gloriosi Corporis mysterium!*'

They heard the cough and footsteps of someone coming down the stairs from the Ultramar's rooms. From the table where he was sitting with Fins, Brinco saw this person's white shoes. Followed by Mariscal himself.

'I thought I heard some kind of prayer. Was that you with the divine words, Rumbo?'

He took a while to respond. And did so uncomfortably, looking askance. 'We were talking about cinema, boss.'

'We were talking about females!' clarified Sergeant Montes. 'Jennifer Jones in *Duel in the Sun*.'

'Now that's a topic of conversation! Personally I would go for the glorious body of St Teresa, by which I mean Aurora Bautista.'

He let them chew over the unexpected billing in order to cap it off, 'Though let's not forget the bodies in *Ben-Hur*!'

The others laughed, but Vargas was confused. '*Ben-Hur*?'

The younger guard followed the movement of Mariscal's arms as he demonstrated the to-and-fro motion of galley rowers.

'Why don't you ever take your gloves off?' asked the guard abruptly.

Sergeant Montes feigned a cough and pretended to pay particular attention to what was going on outside the window. That simpleton Belvís was walking along the road, imitating the sound of a motorbike. *Vroom vroom*. Which was how he went about his errands. Mariscal ignored Vargas' question and instead carried on rowing in a roundabout motion, till he clapped his hands together to signal the end.

'*Mutatis mutandis*. There's no one like John Wayne!'

Rumbo agreed, gestured OK and served him a glass of Johnnie Walker.

'With him and a horse, you can make a film,' Mariscal went on, blessing his statement with a swig. 'You don't even need a woman. What's more, you don't even need a horse. But a weapon, yes. You need a weapon, that's for sure.'

In ceremonial style he clanked the ice cubes against his glass. 'A man's gotta do what a man's gotta do.'

'And keep on doing so for many years!' said Montes, raising his glass.

Brinco stood up and walked towards the front door. This insipid exit drew the men's attention. Rumbo immediately fired a warning shot. 'Víctor, I don't want to see you in the ruins of that school.'

'Lame goes there. I saw him,' replied Brinco, referring to the schoolteacher Barbeito.

'He knows where to step.'

'Your father's right,' said Mariscal solemnly. 'That place is bewitched. Always has been!'

After this, everyone waited for him to add something. Mariscal realised at once that his statement had been a key and not a lock. Instead of bringing the matter to a close, he had just opened or reopened the mystery. He suddenly changed subject, with a mocking expression. He had that ability. One face concealed another. 'Listen, boys. Talking of school, I want to teach you something useful.'

As he addressed the two boys, he winked at the guards. 'Never forget this saying: when you're working, you're not earning any money.'

He chucked a coin, which landed at Brinco's feet. The boy stared at it, with contempt to start with. He didn't even bend down. The group of men carried on watching him. Fins as well, sitting next to him. Through the half-open door the wind danced inside the curtains, not pushing them very far. Finally Brinco bent down and picked up the coin.

Mariscal smiled, turned to the bar and rang the ice cubes in his glass, 'Another spiritual, Rumbo, if you don't mind!'

10

Leda grabbed the door knocker. She liked this hand made of metal and green rust. It was cold and hot at the same time. Then she knocked insistently at the door of the Malpicas' home. Three and one. Three and one. Fins went to answer the door. Nine Moons stared at him. Laughingly to begin with, then more seriously. She had a collection of different expressions. She pulled at him imperiously. 'Come on, move!'

This time she picked a short cut through the old dunes, jumping from side to side to avoid the sea holly. They ran to the top of the primary dune, from where they contemplated the beach's Dantesque spectacle. The sea had now vomited up mannequins, of the kind used in shop windows for displaying the latest fashions. Wooden corpses. Mostly disjointed. The waves nuzzled amputated bodies, loose extremities. Arms, bare feet, heads twisting and turning in the sand.

Nine Moons and Fins trudged their way through the field of casualties, unearthing and lifting up members they then returned to the ground.

They were searching for survivors. Leda finally came across an intact body. A black, female mannequin. She bent down and wiped the sand from its mouth and eyes. Its face had sculptural features and was attractive.

'Pretty, hey?' she said.

The dry sand resembled silver make-up. Fins gazed at this face that was both alive and dead, that seemed to be forming itself as its features emerged. But he didn't say anything.

'Give me a hand, will you?' said Leda, standing up. 'We're going to take this one.'

'Take it? Where?'

Leda didn't answer, but grabbed the mannequin by its ankles. 'Hold it by its shoulders. With tenderness, mind!'

'With tenderness?'

'Just hold it.'

Leda and Fins carried the mannequin along the coastal road, following the shoreline. The girl took the lead, holding the figure by its calves. Fins went behind, supporting the mannequin by its neck. Their laborious walk accompanied by the heaving sea.

What fills the valley now is the sound of a Western trailer. Wind on the back of wind. Shots in the air. A requiem for mannequins. Advancing slowly along the road, in the opposite direction to Fins and Leda, is a car, a Simca 1000, with a roof rack to which is tethered a loudspeaker emitting the trailer, an advert for a film to be shown the following weekend in the cinema Paris-Noitía, at the Ultramar. *For a Few Dollars More*. The way the shots resound in the valley. The wind climbs on top of the wind. That music counting down to the showdown. Rumbo feels happy. Not just because the film is going to fill the cinema, which it is, but on account of this exhilarating ride on horseback, this taking the film out for a spin in the valley. Setting all and sundry on edge. Stunning birds and scarecrows.

Quique Rumbo stopped the car on reaching the mannequin bearers and turned off the cassette blaring out of the loudspeakers. He always gave the impression of being a man of experience. Someone who was used to the unexpected and trained to give a suitable response. And yet, according to Lucho Malpica, Rumbo – Quique Rumbo – had moments when he spat blood. He wound down the car window with a look of curiosity.

'Why don't you get *Los chicos con las chicas*?' Leda began.

'That's a very fine dummy, Nine Moons!' he exclaimed ironically. 'How much do you want for it?'

'It's not for sale,' replied the girl firmly. 'It doesn't have a price.'

This wasn't the first time Rumbo or Fins had heard her sound off like a trader just beginning to bargain. What she did, however, was start walking again with a sudden impulse that took in both Fins and the mannequin.

Rumbo leaned out and shouted from the car window, 'Everything has a price, you know!'

At Chafariz Cross, she took the road leading uphill to the Ultramar. Fins hoped she might agree to sell the dummy after deciding on a price. But to his surprise, she kept going, turning left along a sunken path. She stopped to catch her breath. The two of them were exhausted. But their tiredness was different. His amounted to a dissatisfied fatigue. That dummy was heavy. Weighed like a blasted robot.

'You're not thinking of taking it there, are you?' he asked.

'I am.'

'You're not!'

Leda smiled with steely determination, and lifted up the rigid beauty.

'I am.'

Inside the School of Indians, the blind mannequin made a pair with the one-armed skeleton. They called it a skeleton, though it wasn't exactly that. It was more of an Anatomical Man. You could see the different-coloured organs and muscles, some of which had disappeared over time, starting with the heart, red-painted latex, and the glass eyes. But there he was, the homunculus, complete with bones. It was a question of entering and selecting the spot. One was calling out for the other.

They decided to clean and explore the floor of the world, each in a different direction.

'Where are you, Fins?'

'In the Antarctic. And you?'

'I'm in Polynesia.'

'You're miles away!'

'Just whistle if you want me to come closer.'

Fins didn't wait long. He gave a whistle.

She replied with another whistle, which was better and stronger.

In this way they drew closer. She didn't say so, but walked with her eyes closed. Felt a geographical feature at her feet. Came to a stop. Opened her eyes and looked down.

'Hey, I'm on top of Everest!' she shouted. 'Where are you?'

'In the Amazon.'

'Well, be careful!'

'You too!'

They were interrupted by a creaking of roof tiles. Dust trailed down, along the line of light. A few bats exited the shady zone, flying with the clumsiness of sleepwalkers.

The couple looked up. The noise stopped. The light focused on them. They decided not to worry.

'I'm in . . . Ireland,' she said.

'I'm in Cuba.'

'Now we have to be really careful,' said Leda. 'We're going to cross the Tenebrous Sea.'

They approached each other. Met. Felt. Touched with their hands. The hands are for touching. They embraced. When they started to kiss, another, louder noise was heard coming from the ceiling.

Leda and Fins, half blinded by the dust, looked up again. Brinco popped his head through the crater, imitating the sound of an owl: 'Twit twoooooo!'

The intruder expelled a gobbet of spit, which sank to the floor next to the standing couple.

'Pig Island!' shouted Leda.

'There's nothing that can't be eaten!' he replied. Then they heard him moving off across the tiles.

'We'd better leave. He could bring the whole roof down.'

He stopped himself because Leda was staring at him, gently wiping the dust off his shoulders.

'Don't worry, nothing's going to come down.'

Nine Moons surveyed the map of Fins Malpica's face with her fingers.

'Arctic, Iceland, Galicia, Azores, Cape Verde . . .'

Fins is now seated at the teacher's desk, to the right of the blind mannequin and the one-armed skeleton. Pretending to type. Banging on keys that move a carriage without paper.

Nine Moons is holding a book. She opened it to have a look, but started turning the pages and is now absorbed in her reading.

'What are you reading?'

'It has lice marks.'

'Did they eat all the letters?'

'Just type.'

'I'm not sure I can. I don't have any paper.'

'That doesn't matter, stupid! Look, type. "All is mute silense . . ."'

'Shouldn't it be "silence" with a "c"?'

'No, it says "silense" with an "s". It must be for a reason.'

11

The parish priest climbed into the pulpit and, before speaking, tapped the microphone with a mixture of caution and shyness until several smiling faces nodded in his direction. It was working. At which point Don Marcelo said that we all more or less knew that God was eternal and infinite. He lasts for ever and is omnipresent, knows no limits. Which is why he is said to have invented human beings, so he had somebody to attend to the minor details. Somebody, so to speak, who could use the Decimal System. Who'd look after the smaller things. Such as changing broken roof tiles. Unblocking drains. Watching the introduction of novelties that make all our lives more bearable. 'To give free rein to the spirit, one must keep an eye on worldly matters. Which is why it is so important to recognise the progress represented by the outdoor speakers we are using for the first time today owing to the kind donation of our fellow parishioner Tomás Brancana, known to all and sundry as Mariscal the Marshal' – though obviously he didn't say this – 'to whom we owe other improvements in this church of St Mary, such as the recent repairs to the roof. One day such generosity will be repaid,' etc., etc. And Mariscal, who had Dona Guadalupe to his right, and to his left the couple formed by Rumbo and Sira, responded with a reverential bow. Don Marcelo, with the increasing confidence supplied by new technology, after his initial nerves, gradually spurred himself on as he realised, indeed felt, that his voice was filling the temple, spreading across the whole valley, climbing the mountainsides and crashing into the sea over at Cape Cons. Even the pagans, to avoid using a stronger word, however much they tried, would never be able to bar this outburst of the spirit. And as he gained in both potency and dominion, he also felt he was gaining in rhetorical quality, in eloquence, and Mariscal himself, a connoisseur of such things, was moved to lift his head and prick up his ears. Because of this, and because it was time, the priest took it upon himself to discuss the mystery of the Holy Trinity. 'In many images,' he said, 'the Supreme Being appears as a venerable old man. And we can all recognise the figure of his Son on the Cross. But then there's the most complex person. The third person. The Holy Spirit. What is the Holy Spirit like?'

At this point Belvís unexpectedly jumped up and whirled his arms like wings. 'It's me! It's me!'

The simpleton had been sitting in the pew for young people. Next to Brinco from the Ultramar. They spent a lot of time together, because Brinco enjoyed his company. And treated him well. Could even be said to be fond of him. Always had been. Which might be why he smiled. Others turned to look at Belvís in surprise, but the priest decided to ignore him. This was a day to remember. Everything was going swimmingly. The speakers were working. So he picked up from where he'd left off, with an explanation of the Holy Spirit.

Belvís did the same. Whirled his arms as if he was going to fly, like one of those wading birds that need a run-up in order to take off. 'It's me! It's me!'

I remember it well because it was the day the outdoor speakers were first used. The priest couldn't take any more, and from the pulpit, without realising that his words were being broadcast over the whole valley, as far as the sea, blurted out,

'That's right, yes. The Holy Spirit is everywhere. But that doesn't give you an excuse to fool around!'

Several adults went over to where Belvís was, and he was forced to leave. He never returned to church. I'm told that in St Mary's, during Mass, whenever the priest makes reference to the Holy Spirit, there are still some who spontaneously turn around and glance at the spot where Belvís was, moving his arms like wings: 'It's me! It's me!'

He stayed in Noitía for a few more years. He'd run errands, take fish and shellfish to the restaurants, goods to old people who were unable to fend for themselves, always gadding about on his imaginary motorbike.

'Will you be long, Belvís?'

'No, I'm on the Montesa.'

Vroom vroom.

He ended up in the loony bin in Conxo. By which I mean the psychiatric hospital. But I don't think he was mad either then or now. He had no father, and suffered a lot when his mother died. When he was a child, his mother looked after him as best she could. In abject misery. The child walked around half naked, without nappies, his willy and bits hanging out in the wind. Which meant he did his necessities wherever he felt like it. One day he chose as a firing range the porch of a neighbour living in the Big House. She had plants, begonias and so on, it seemed like a good enough place and he dropped his entire payload. He needed to go and so he went. But it so happened that the neighbour spotted him and gave him a real spanking. He returned home in floods of tears. When his mother found out, she took him in her arms, went to the Big House and called to the neighbour until she appeared on the balcony. Then Belvís' mother lifted him up, his naked bum in the air, kissed him on his buttocks and shouted out, 'What a bottom, what a blessing!' Now that is love.

He was so taken aback when his mother died that he lost all his voices, even the Montesa. He'd always been good at voices, ever since he was a little boy. A man or a woman's. He could make puppets out of anything, out of cardboard and rags, and get them to talk. He did a fine impersonation of the singer Four Winds, who starred at local festivities and had this nickname because of four missing teeth. He would sing, 'Let the boat leave the beach, it will come back again. There is his lover, she is constant, constant, constant, constant . . . in her feelings towards him.' This repetition of the word 'constant' occurred to him as a boy and people couldn't stop laughing. He had that ability. His best voice was definitely Charlie the Kid, by which I mean Charlie Chaplin with a Buenos Aires accent. He was good at that. The puppet and voice were all he inherited from a great-uncle who came back from Argentina to die.

Then things changed at the hospital. They let him out. Well, they discharged him, but then they let him come back. On account of the Kid, he says, who feels better there. At weekends he hits the road, a kind of one-man orchestra, out with his puppet to make a few pesetas. He's very good, though that is hardly surprising. So much time talking to themselves. That must be why Víctor Rumbo hired him to perform at that club of his, the Vaudeville. So he could earn himself a few pesetas. He probably did it as a joke. But I don't think that was any place for Belvís. People who go there are after something else. And I don't just mean the scroungers and hangers-on, as the Kid would say. That's the thing about Brinco, he was always like that. Attracted to strange people like Chelín or Belvís. Those he loved, he loved a lot. But those he hated, he hated with enthusiasm.

* * *

I'm getting ahead of myself.

Now I can see them as children. They're playing football in a flat area of the old dunes, halfway between A de Meus and Noitía. A good place to use as a pitch. The dunes protect them from the north-east wind and act as a wall to stop the ball running down to the sea. You have to see Belvís, who is broadcasting the game as if it was a match between football legends, in which he himself is an ace. And now they're going to take penalties. Chelín is in goal. He's just made a superb save from Brinco. He's euphoric, having just stopped Fins' pile-driver. And now Leda is running up. It's her turn to shoot. She takes aim, but has to stop all of a sudden. Chelín abandons his post.

'Where the hell are you going?' asks Leda, feeling annoyed.

'Women don't take penalties.'

'Since when?'

Belvís darts and swoops about them. Continuing to commentate in his exaggerated style. 'There's a moment of great tension in the stadium of Sporting Noitía. Nine Moons has got in the way of Chelín the goalkeeper. Chelín's not happy about it. Attention. Fins the referee is having to intervene,' etc., etc.

'Tell the truth, Chelín,' barks Brinco, who finds the whole situation very amusing. 'You're shitting yourself.'

'No, it's just I'm not a homo.'

In a rage, Leda picks up speed and drives the ball with all her might. But Chelín shows his reflexes, makes an arc in the air and stops it. He embraces the ball, lying on the ground, his face in the sand, smiling, victorious and out of breath.

'See? I'm not afraid. It's my hidden powers.'

'You fool,' she says. 'I've always stood up for you. Now you're going to have to kiss my feet.'

12

They were always there, as volunteers, to help turn the cinema into a dance hall. Rumbo would give them a few cold drinks as a tip. And let them take the bits of celluloid he cut in order to splice the film when it was broken. To tell the truth, they all ended up in the hands of Fins, who was crazy about stills. He'd put together his own collection, and would order all those fragments of cinema at home. One memorable day Rumbo came back to A de Meus, the sea heaving in the background, with *Moby Dick* and Captain Ahab, Gregory Peck, in his pocket. That was several years ago, though the film was still included each season because it was one of his favourites. He had his obsessions, one of which was Spencer Tracy. He showed *Captains Courageous* more than once, and the film about the life of Thomas Alva Edison. When Edison invented the filament of light, all the audience applauded. But Rumbo's admiration for Tracy could be summed up in a single gesture. He'd take his arm out of the sleeve of his jacket, which hung down like a one-armed man's, and declare the title with great exaggeration: '*Bad Day at Black Rock*!' He always said the name of that accursed place, Black Rock, with a croak in his voice. His attraction for this actor may have had something to do with the fact that Rumbo looked like him. Whenever anybody pointed this out, he would reply ironically, 'Or vice versa!'

That said, the films he liked best were Westerns. Followed by gangster movies. From time to time there would be an Italian film and he'd attend the projection with the bearing of a navigation officer on the bridge. He'd declare, 'Too much truth for the cinema.' An opinion he let slide into the cans when he was putting away the rolls of film, as if he had no one else to talk to. 'That Magnani puts them all to shame.' He definitely didn't like films with swordsmen, an opinion he shared with his boss, Mariscal. Fins knew this, having heard a curse that was regularly used in the Ultramar: 'I shit on the Three Musketeers and Cardinal Richelieu!' Rumbo's theory was that, in the age of firearms, it was backward to make films with steel. And, together with the audience, he celebrated the progress that saw Indians equipped with Winchester rifles. 'That gives them a fighting chance.' Though in the end they just died more and more quickly.

Today, as night fell after the afternoon's session, the sound of shots being fired, Clint Eastwood's horse on the move and the lazy flight of scraps of dried grass all descended into the dunes' desert. Rumbo whistled the catchy tune to *For a Few Dollars More* and so set the rhythm for the methodical, simple transformation that turned the cinema into a dance hall. All the lights went on, emphasising the colours of the garlands. Brinco, Leda and Fins placed the chairs against the wall and swept the floor, though Belvís was the quickest, riding his noisy, invisible Montesa. On the stage they let down a velvety black curtain that covered the screen. The musicians entered without a sound. Sometimes you weren't even sure they were there until they took out their instruments and began to warm up. Rumbo arranged a buffet at the other end of the hall, opposite the stage, in a dimly lit area. The band of musicians today included two guitarists. Today was special. Sira was going to sing. She hadn't sung since the previous New Year's Eve. It wasn't that she was responsible for livening up the dance; she wasn't even the main voice. But she'd always come out to sing two or three *fados*. And this was a starlit moment. As the schoolteacher Barbeito used to say, there were two nights after listening to Sira Portosalvo. The night that froze the sense of unease. And the night that gave it shelter.

Everybody was waiting. The eldest were sitting down on either side of the hall. In front of them, couples dancing. The youngest in the middle and at the back. While the musicians played *merengues* and *cumbias*, a group led by Brinco mucked about with Leda and Fins, pushing them so that they would dance together. The girl was wearing a printed summer dress and turning round and round. Fins felt annoyed. He had his arms crossed and defended himself with his elbows against the others, who jumped around at the end of 'La piragua'. The moment Sergeant Montes and Vargas the guard came in, a few of the elders sitting down stopped talking and glanced in their direction. The guards surveyed the scene and headed for the bar, where Rumbo made sure they were well attended.

Then Sira came in. Wearing a black shawl and large silver hoop earrings inlaid with jet. She looked around, her head raised, then removed her shoes.

'I would like to dedicate the first song of the night to the dance's finest couple,' she said. 'The one from the Civil Guard!'

She'd done this before. No one was surprised. Sergeant Montes smiled with satisfaction. Hungered after the singer. And the *fado* began, 'I had the keys of life, but didn't open the doors where happiness lived', at which point all the other details lost their meaning. Sira, Sira's voice, captivated every nook and cranny, every glance. The door of the dance hall opened and in came Mariscal, who walked diagonally without taking in the stage. At the buffet, he gestured in greeting to the guards with his hat. Whispered something to Rumbo, who nodded and offered the guards a second drink. Imported whisky. Johnnie Walker. They were grateful and raised their glasses in a toast.

And while Sira sang 'Chaves da vida', Brinco left the dance hall. Followed by Leda and Fins.

Brinco ran towards the beach, abandoned the dance hall, in an attempt to escape his mother's charming voice. He realised there were two hangers-on. Stopped and turned around with an angry expression. 'What? Always sniffing around my bottom.'

'We belong here as much as you!' said Leda defiantly.

'You really never stop talking. My mother's right.'

Brinco knew how to wound with his tongue, but this time he realised that his last sentence was an arrow aimed at himself. He set off running. Leda's voice chased after him, 'Well, look who's doing the talking, mummy's boy!'

The whore who gave birth to her, he thought, how well she knew how to hit the spot. He came to the beached boat where two men were waiting, the veteran Carburo and younger Inverno. Garbled the message, tripping on his words because of all the running and the annoyance caused by the others, like carrying along a string of cans. 'Rumbo says you can start unloading!'

'Unloading what?' asked Carburo. The boy needed training.

'The tuna, of course!'

The other two approached, running.

'And these two Martians?' asked Inverno.

'Oh, these two will work for free.'

The two men laughed. 'Well, aren't we the lucky ones?'

The group started walking with Carburo at the front. His

large head, his body slightly bowed. A sculpted figure wounding the night. Leda heard what Brinco said to Inverno and reacted bravely. 'Free, my arse.'

'She's a wild one,' said Inverno. 'That's it, girl, make sure you protect your interests.'

In a whisper, to Brinco, 'That girl, in a few years' time, will be pure dynamite.'

From the end of the breakwater, a man signals in Morse with a torch. Another replies from a boat not far out at sea. It's summer and the sea is calm. Shortly afterwards there is the sound of a nautical engine, and the silhouette of a fishing boat comes into view.

The fishing boat docks. Heavily laden, fore and aft, with large shapes covered in nets and other fishing tackle, such as buoys and creels. When the sailors remove the camouflage, cardboard boxes containing smuggled tobacco are revealed. Mussel-raft blond. More people have arrived, mostly men, but also some women, moving between the darkness of the nearby pine groves and the light of the moon, which illuminates the ramp of the old harbour.

A Mercedes turns up and out gets Mariscal. All the carriers take up position, quickly forming a well-spaced human line. Mariscal follows their movements from the promontory. He has a good panoramic view, but he also knows that he is visible. Raised in the night. The mouth that talks.

'Everything all right, Gamboa?'

'Everything OK, boss.'

'Carburo, get these people moving!'

'Everybody listen. At full speed. In order and in silence. There's no need to worry. The guards are still at the dance.'

One of the women taking part in the procession starts singing a ballad, 'Did you dance, Carolina? Yes, I danced! Tell me who you danced with! I danced with the colonel!' and Mariscal smiles. Orders quiet. Claps his hands in the air.

'Now let's get to work. It's not true that God gives time for nothing.'

The line begins transferring the packages in absolute silence, from the ramp to the old salting factory, a sombre stone building of a single storey. There are about twenty of them. They work with diligence and normality, except for the children, whose sweat shows they're doing it for the first time. When it's all over, Mariscal pays everybody in person. Listens to the murmured litany of appreciation. When it's Brinco's turn, he grabs him by the shoulders with satisfaction.

'This time you've earned yourself a Catholic Monarchs!'

Then he whispers in his ear so that only Brinco can hear. Does so with a paternal smile. 'Don't bring volunteers without telling me first, got it?'

'But they stick to me!'

'I know, they're just stray dogs.'

'Boss, the guards are coming!'

'Not to worry, Inverno. They come when they have to.'

Sergeant Montes emerges from the pine groves. Vargas quickly takes up position behind him.

'Nobody move!' shouts Montes. 'What's going on here?'

Nobody says a word. Mariscal waits. He knows how to let the gears of time engage.

'Forgive me, sergeant,' he says finally. 'Would you mind if we spoke alone for a moment?'

Once they're at a certain distance, Mariscal casually drops something on the ground. 'Sergeant, I do believe you dropped two notes. Two green ones, *sensu stricto.*'

The sergeant glances at the ground. Yes, there are two thousand-peseta notes.

'Excuse me, sir. *Sensu stricto*, I do believe I dropped at least ten.'

And Mariscal proceeds to free the other notes, as if he's already made the calculation.

13

Back from unloading the tobacco, Fins placed his thousand-peseta note on top of the oilskin tablecloth. His mother, Amparo, put down her knitting in surprise. His father was listening to the radio closely, making an ear trumpet with the palm of his hand. Cassius Clay, newly named Muhammad Ali, had just been stripped of his world heavyweight title due to his refusal to be inducted into the military during the Vietnam War. Lucho Malpica turned down the volume and jumped to his feet. 'What's this money?'

'Mr Rumbo gave it to me for cleaning the vats.'

'He never pays that much for cleaning vats.'

'Well, it was about time he paid more,' said Fins uneasily.

Lucho Malpica waved the note in front of his son's face. 'Don't ever lie to me!'

The boy remained silent, feeling uncomfortable, chewing over the words of before and afterwards.

'The worst lie of all is silence.'

'Mr Mariscal gave it to me,' said the boy eventually. 'I helped unload some tobacco.'

'That's more like it. More than I can earn fighting with the sea for a whole damn week!'

Now two of them were chewing over the past and present.

'Have you any idea how that bastard got rich?'

'Wasn't it in Cuba, before the revolution?'

'In Cuba?'

Lucho Malpica had always dodged the issue of Mariscal. He even avoided saying his name, would take a roundabout route in the conversation, like someone sidestepping a turd. But now the issue had been blown open. And the unstoppable destination was irony.

'What did he do in Cuba? What was his job?'

'Wasn't he a boxing promoter, organising fights, with a cinema or something? I don't know, Dad, that's what I heard.'

'Selling peanuts in a cone. In Cuba? That guy never set foot in America.'

Lucho Malpica realised it wasn't going to be easy to tell the story of Mariscal. Even for him, who was of the same generation, there were large areas of shade. Mariscal vanished and came back. With a shadow that grew and grew, and made him more powerful.

'After the war, his parents worked on the black market. They'd always been involved in smuggling.'

'Everyone was involved in smuggling,' said Amparo suddenly. 'Where there's a border, there's smuggling. Even I, as a girl, went over one time with a flat stomach and came back pregnant, God forgive me. I took over sugar and three pairs of high-heeled shoes and came back with coffee and silk. I did it once and never again. It wasn't a sin, but it was a crime. They once shot a Portuguese kid who didn't stop when he was supposed to. He was carrying a pair of shoes. His mother came to see where he'd fallen. There was still a trace of blood. She kneeled down, took out a scarf and wiped it up. Didn't leave a speck. Shouted, "I don't want any to remain here!"'

'What you're talking about was survival,' said Malpica. 'There were people who hired themselves out, smuggled things in their bellies . . .'

'That's what I was like,' replied Amparo. 'Though I lit a candle to St Barbara first, so it wouldn't thunder.'

'What I'm talking about wasn't to feed people's hunger. The Brancanas ran an organisation. Like today. There were lots of part-time smugglers. Smugglers for hire. Women with bellies. But the way they made their money was with wolfram. Then oil, petrol, medicine, meat. And weapons. Whatever was needed. And the mother, who'd been a maid, when she went up in the world, got it into her head that one of her children could be a bishop or a cardinal. Someone ironically suggested they could be a marshal. And she replied with evident glee, why not? A cardinal or a marshal. Which is how Mariscal the Marshal got his name. You know how quick people are on the uptake round here. So she decided to send her precious boy to the seminary. In Tui. He was no man's fool. Always a smart one. And even then he was good at solving problems. His own and others'. He got a private room in the seminary and turned it into a marketplace. Of course there was the odd priest who shared in the profits. And that's where he met Don Marcelo, who was also a student.'

'Don Marcelo is of a different vintage,' intervened Amparo.

'All saints are endowed with manhood,' said Malpica.

'Don't talk for the fair, Lucho! A good speaker is one who stays silent.'

'I talk in round terms, keep nothing silent from the sun's son . . . Oh, enough of that! It went from mouth to ear, as they say around here.'

'Then why did he leave the seminary?' asked Fins.

Malpica smiled at Amparo, seeking her complicity in the story.

'He must have been there for three years. When he's drunk, he says it was because he wanted to become pope. What he doesn't deny is that he started a roaring trade in foodstuffs. Had a grocery store beneath his bed! There was cold and hunger. And he took advantage of the situation. He had coffee liqueur and Western novels. He always was a competent supplier. But I don't think they chucked him out because of that. The trouble is, a chalice and image were stolen during a pilgrimage he went on as an acolyte. They found the chalice under his mattress. Nothing was ever known about the Virgin. Though he always had a taste for virgins. The family covered it up, compensated the Church with money. It all remained under wraps. As did what came afterwards.'

Fins' father turned to the radio and slowly moved the dial in an effort to tune into some frequency. For radio waves as well, A de Meus was a place in shadow. Fins was afraid his struggle with the static would put paid to the story about Mariscal.

'So what happened afterwards that people don't know?'

'He went to prison.'

'Mariscal was in prison?'

'That's right. Tomás Brancana, Mariscal, was in prison. And not as a visitor either. He started by helping out in the family business, which was well established. But he was ambitious, and he found another, more lucrative activity. He got himself a tanker, but didn't transport oil or wine. He transported people! He had his agents, his *engajadores*, in Portugal. The emigrants gave him everything they had in order to get to France. And during the night, on top of some mountain, he'd tell them to get out and shout, "You're in France, for crying out loud. *La France*, remember! Run, run!" Of course it wasn't France. He left them sometimes on this side of the border, lost on some snowy mountaintop, without food or money, dying of cold. One day there was a collision, an accident, and they had no choice but to declare it was him since he was the one who'd been driving. He went to prison, but not for long. Nobody knows. I'm not sure there was even a court case. Evil knows how to float. It floats like fuel, just beneath the surface. And he had a tidy sum of money set aside. And partners! So when people say he was in America, you can give that country this name: the clink on Prince Street in Vigo!'

Fins Malpica recalled the first time he'd listened to Mariscal up close. That sermon he'd spouted in the School of Indians when they discovered the stash of whisky. He tried to remember his Latin phrases, the rhetoric they were couched in. *Learn that and you've gained half a life. The rest is also very simple.* Oculos habent, et non videbunt. *They have eyes, and see not.* Aures habent, et non audient. *They have ears, and hear not.*

They have mouths, and speak not.

'You'll be thinking I know a lot about a man I never talk about. Well, you're right. And do you know how I know? Because I also tried to get to France . . . Later on, when I could have gone there legally, I didn't want to. I still had icicles on my beard from the first time. That man only ever did one good thing in his life, which is when he burned his hands in the School of Indians. They say it was on account of the books, but it was because of the desiccated animals. Even better. Desiccated makes you feel more sorry for them. Not even the fox got away. That's what he did. God knows why.'

Fins stared for a moment at the burn scars on his father's hands. Lucho Malpica rolled his son's note into a ball and flicked it across the table. The ball veered to one side and came to a halt in front of Amparo.

'She's also partly to blame,' said Amparo suddenly.

'Who?' asked Lucho.

'That loudmouth who drives him crazy, Antonio's daughter. You should say something to Antonio. You spend all that time together out fishing.'

Lucho glanced at his son and then at his wife. They should

know by now that sorrows on a boat were for spitting into the sea. 'What am I supposed to tell him? That he should keep her tied up at home?'

'That wouldn't be a bad idea. She's far too wild. She's always going barefoot. Like a beggar or something.'

'It has nothing to do with us,' remarked Lucho bitterly. He could barely hide it when a topic of conversation annoyed him. 'Let her walk however she likes.'

What bothered him even more, however, was a breakdown in the domestic order. And so he adopted a more conciliatory tone. 'We do talk, from time to time. But you can't touch Antonio's daughter. She's the most precious thing he has in the world. He'd do anything for her.'

14

Malpica has a small motorboat which he uses for coastal fishing. It handles well, is definitely seaworthy, but Lucho and Antonio Hortas rarely stray from their familiar marks. They have their points of reference along the coast, the main one being Cape Cons. With these marks, their eyes trace invisible lines, the co-ordinates of their sardine shoals for fishing. Underwater places that almost never leave them empty-handed.

This time they go further out. Even the seabirds seem surprised by their new direction and abandon them. The boat bobs up and down, in unfamiliar territory. The men are two grafts who resist the swaying of the boat impassively. It's Malpica who decides where they're going, who acts as captain from time to time. And now they're headed north. Antonio neither asks anything nor makes any comment. He's one of those who respect silences. They pass Sálvora. Head towards the outer sea. The cormorants on Death Coast peer at them with the look of medi-eval sentinels. Lucho Malpica still hasn't said a word, but Antonio can hear his nasal hoarseness, his sibilant pout, those two murmurs that compete in his friend's silences.

The captain opens a wickerwork basket lined with canvas. Antonio knows what's in there. He knows Malpica visited the Ultramar the previous night. He didn't enter the bar, but he saw him arrive on his 'little horse', as he calls his Ducati. He must have gone in through the shop door. The attendant called to Rumbo through the hatch which communicates with the bar. And the barman disappeared for a while. Then Antonio heard Malpica leave. Heard the motorbike. The put-put of the engine. The annoyance of old engines at having to start up again. They left in daylight, too early. When Fins came round with the countermand that they would be heading out to sea, Antonio knew the fishing would be special.

He's seeing all this now, with absolute clarity, in causal sequences. He may not have heard the engine from the bar. It may be the engine on the boat, its laborious bad temper, providing a soundtrack to his memory.

The sticks are wrapped in an immaculate white cloth inside the basket. Even there he's being too careful, observes Antonio. Dynamite doesn't like being thought about so much. Antonio remembers seeing maimed people. The idea has to get back to the hands. If the idea stops to think, it doesn't reach the hands. That's when you get injured people. Amputees.

'Leave that to me, Lucho.'

'Why?' he says, turning around with an angry expression.

'You haven't the experience.'

He was going to say, 'You don't know how.' Like someone saying, 'You don't know how to fuck.'

Antonio doesn't mind. He knows others use dynamite. The sea takes whatever's thrown at it, etc., etc. But deep down he's annoyed that Malpica has given in. Has lit the damn fuse.

'What science is there in this, Antonio?' says Lucho uneasily, waving the stick in his hand. He's on the starboard side and heads towards the bow.

'To start with, it doesn't have a very long fuse!' shouts Antonio.

Malpica turns around. See? Do you see what's happening? The idea has got caught in his head, entangled in the brambles en route to his damn consciousness, and isn't going to reach his hand in time.

'What's that?' asks Malpica.

The idea doesn't get there. It's the dynamite which has decided to explode. And explodes.

Fins starts throwing stones at the sky. There are so many seagulls he has the impression he hasn't hit any of them. Then he takes it out on the sea. Looks for the flattest pebbles and skilfully hurls them by arching his body. Like a discus thrower. His initial intention is for the stones to skim the surface of the sea. To jump on the back of the waves. After that, he doesn't mind. Small, big. In a fury. Let the stones explode. It's the sea's fault. That generous, greedy giant. That crazy lunatic. 'The sea prefers the brave ones and that's why she takes them first,' says the priest at the funeral. Everyone nods. They all wear expressions that suggest agreement with that part of the sermon. Enough said. What happened happened. It was written in the stars. It was out of his hands. Fins thinks he's being looked at askance. Are you brave too? Are you like your father? Yes, there is compassion in their gaze, but also a hint of suspicion. He never put to sea with his father. It was time he lent a hand. Are they in on the secret? Do they realise he's not fit for the sea?

His father was certainly brave. You could see that when he carried the cross. A first-rate Christ. Verisimilar. Did the priest say that, or was it an echo emanating from his mind? Do they know he suffers from the *petit mal*, has absences?

Like now.

He can see his father shaving himself. The mirror, which

has a diagonal crack, reflects two faces. His mother asking. Not asking.

'And that?'

'It has time to grow. From now until Easter.'

Without a beard, his father looks strange. Like another. The reverse of what he is. All the bones on his face appear bereft of bandages.

15

The radio is broadcasting the Holy Rosary. The litany sounds sometimes when the radio is turned on at dusk, but it never usually gets a response. Not from the mouths. Possibly from the intentional beating of the knitting needles. Fins rereads a piece of headed paper:

LA DIVINA PASTORA
NAVY SOCIAL INSTITUTION
School for Sea Orphans
Sanlúcar de Barrameda (Cádiz)

Is that someone knocking at the door? Fins stirs in discomfort. Stands up. Looks at the radio. The lamp on the dial which gleams with the intensity of a beacon in the open sea. The trembling of the cloth covering the loudspeaker like skin. The memory of his father's fingers fishing in the short waves, tautening the dial like a fishing line. He's listening carefully. Turns to him with a smile. 'Do you know what he said? "No Viet Cong ever called me nigger."' Fins glances at his mother.

'It's the static,' says Amparo. 'Pray with me. It won't hurt!'

He should go to see her. Her dad is still in hospital. All his skin burned off. Eight hours being beaten by the sea. From rock to rock. He has pneumonia as well. He should go to see her.

'I should go and see Antonio.'

'He's still in the municipal hospital. I'll go. He'll get over it. He was saved.'

Her silence finishes the sentence: 'He was saved, but your father wasn't.'

'At least now he may have more luck with her.'

'What do you mean?'

'Haven't you seen her? Riding around on the other's motorbike, in a tight embrace. You have your head in the clouds.'

'Brinco was given a motorbike. He's trying it out. What's wrong with that? The other day he took me for a ride.'

'But she's a woman. She's a woman by now! She has to look after her father. She can't be a source of gossip.'

Fins has always had the impression that his mother has various voices. Two at least. She keeps the rough one for Nine Moons. She sometimes tries to be polite, but when Leda comes to visit, she always ends up falling silent. It's too much for her.

'It's the last night. Pray a little with me, child.'

Lord, have mercy . . . Lord, have mercy.

Christ, hear us . . . Christ, hear us.

Fins resists, moves his lips, but is unable to find his voice. Slowly he notices how the saliva kneads his words. Feels well. The litany wets its feet, steps on the soft sand, closes its eyes. Opens them. He thinks he hears someone knocking at the door again. His look pulls him in that direction. He suddenly stands up. Opens the door. The wind in the fig tree. The screeching of the sea. His mother's rosary. Outside in, inside out, everything sounds like a single litany. The unmoved hand. Made of metal and green rust. From the *Liverpool*. He'd like to be able to pull it off. To take it with him. Three and one.

Holy Virgin of virgins, pray for us.

Mother of divine grace, pray for us.

'Tomorrow you have to get up early. To arrive in time for the train, you have to catch the first bus. Why don't you go to bed? I'm not sleepy.'

And she gets the expression of her feelings messed up. She wants to cry, but comes out with a twisted smile instead. 'It's the night of the widow.'

'Good night, mother.'

'Son . . .'

'Yes?'

'Don't forget to take It.'

It's funny. His mother never wants to call things, medicines or illnesses, by their name. She doesn't even call dynamite dynamite. She says 'the thing that killed him'. In his case, Luminal is 'the thing for absences'.

'I'll send It to you every month. Dr Fonseca promised me. Your father spoke to him. And he gave his word.'

Fins climbs the stairs to the landing where the bedrooms are. Meanwhile his mother takes up her work with the cushion and needles for making lace. She carries on listening to the rosary on the radio, but stops murmuring the litany as her movement with the needles accelerates. The geometry of lace starts to confuse lines. Sound confuses rhythm. In his room, Fins hurries to open the window. The humming and screeching of the sea come in. He feels the itching of salty darkness in his eyes. Closes it again. The fig tree's resentful shadows slice the window all through the night.

Dawn cannot lift its feet due to the weight of the storm clouds. But the sea is almost calm, its blue so cold it gives the slow curls of foam the texture of ice. Fins walks along the coastal road, following the shoreline. He crosses the bridge at Lavandeira da Noite and sits down to wait at Chafariz Cross, where the bus stops. As he was walking, he watched the women gathering shellfish on the sandbank. The more distant ones looked like amphibian creatures with water around their thighs. From the window of the bus, before leaving, Fins Malpica glances at the beach for the last time, through the filter of condensation. Now rosy-fingered dawn clears a way with daggers of light. All barefoot women are Nine Moons. And he opens the book at the page about Argonauts with empty eyes.

16

'You believe in that naive contention that a world in which every-body read and everybody was cultured would be better. Imagine a place like Uz, but where every house had a library and every bar its own circle of readers. Whenever there was a crime, it was carried out with style and criminals were vested with the prosody of a Macbeth or a Meursault.'

'I think we haven't done too badly as far as the last point goes. In the history of Spain, people have killed with great eloquence. The greatest poets presented Philip IV with an anthology of poems for killing a bull with a harquebus.'

They were in the Ultramar, in the chiaroscuro of the table in the corner, next to the window. They chatted there almost every day, in the evening, when the old teacher Basilio Barbeito had finished school. He lived at the Ultramar. During the winter season, apart from the odd visitor, he was the only guest. Dr Fonseca had a house in town, near his surgery. For the married couple, Sira in particular, who prepared the food and washed the clothes, the schoolteacher, with the passing of time, was just another member of the family. He didn't seem to have anywhere else to go. Though he did receive lots of letters in the Ultramar, some of them with the red, white and blue stripes of airmail. He was a poet. Without books. But he scattered his poems across the globe, in minor magazines. And he had been working for some time on a *Dictionary of Euphemisms and Dysphemisms in the Latin Languages*.

'Barbeito, I fail to understand, with everything you've witnessed, everything that's happened, how you can continue to scrabble about for sparks of hope.'

'You're the one fighting against death. I have no other choice but to write poems in an attempt to divert his attention.'

'Fighting against death? He always get his sums right,' murmured Dr Fonseca. 'Always gets what he wants. If this one isn't ready, he takes someone he wasn't supposed to.'

'You should patent that law.'

'Oh, it was patented a long time ago. I do what I have to. Something I find increasingly tiresome. You're the one who has a redeeming vocation. That's damaging. Your poetry promotes well-being, as heating does.'

The schoolteacher listened to the other man's observation with a triumphant sneer. 'And they say that poetry has no uses! When I had lots of energy, I used to write poems of despair. Now that I'm old, I've become hymnic, celebratory, pantheistic, fabulous. For me a poem is like stretching out your hand. Fonseca, you know more about the arrow than I do.'

'What arrow?'

'The arrow of terrible beauty.'

'I think about the body's text from time to time, yes. You'll find there all the different genres: Eros, crime, travel, Gothic terror . . . But I have been castrated by scientific puritanism. I lack the courage to turn the leucocyte into a hero, as Ramón y Cajal did: "The wandering leucocyte opens a gap in the vascular wall and deserts the blood for the conjunctive regions." Now that is epic!'

'Don't fool yourself. You could be another Chekhov,' said

Barbeito suddenly. 'Why don't you write, why don't you express what you have inside you before it explodes?'

'Because I haven't the balls.'

'Fonseca, my friend, allow me a solemn reproach. Humanity is lessened by the silence of one who knows.'

When Basilio Barbeito deliberately adopted a grandiloquent tone, with comic seriousness, not without double meaning, Dr Fonseca would play along with his rhetoric game and respond with a melancholy verse taken from a poem by Rosalía de Castro, which he turned into a mocking refrain: 'The tremor of little bells, Barbeito!'

But not this time. This time he added, 'I haven't the balls or the authority. I can't write what I have to. Do you remember when the herdsman comes across Oedipus the King? "I stand upon the perilous edge of speech." That's what the old herdsman says, more or less. And Oedipus replies, "And I of hearing, but I still must hear!" What a magnificent couplet!'

The doctor would have loved to preserve the process passing through his mind in Ehrlich's methylene blue. He'd been held in St Anthony's Castle in Coruña during the military uprising. A horde of captive men, unaware whether all this was going to end in tragedy or a passing kind of stupor. But before it was dark, an officer arrived with his assistant, a new recruit. The officer ordered this soldier, who sometimes acted as his secretary, to read out a list. A list of people. That's all it was. The whole bay fell quiet. A series of names and surnames. No explanation about what would be their destination, just the abstract idea of a 'transfer'. 'Get ready for a transfer.' The word had blushed with the shame of such a terrible euphemism. And then Luís Fonseca heard his name. He kept silent. Couldn't remember how long that silence lasted. The soldier repeated his name, louder this time. And out of the crowd of people appeared a man. He was older than the doctor. About ten years older. Fonseca later found out he'd been a mechanic. He'd never heard of him, they weren't related, but they had the same name. 'I'm Luís Fonseca,' he said with gritty determination. He was killed that same night. Now that was a classic question of the Double.

'But I'm not a herdsman, nor am I Oedipus,' remarked Dr Fonseca. 'I am not upon the perilous edge, nor do I have anything to say.'

'You belong to the mysterious lineage of Dictinius,' said the schoolteacher. 'In the sixth century, he wrote *The Pound* in praise of the number twelve. He later burned it, leaving only that great saying in the history of Galicia: "Swear, forswear, and reveal not the secret!"'

Mariscal had come over and sat down at the table, as he did on other evenings. In time to hear the resignation in Fonseca's voice. He had a psalm on the tip of his tongue, but there was too much bitterness in the doctor's silence to joke around.

'What about you, Mr Mariscal?' asked Barbeito in an attempt to lighten the mood.

'I'm Unamunian!'

Normally he'd have left it at that, an outlandish statement hanging in the air. But on this occasion he decided it was prudent to expand on his thesis. 'I'm of the opinion that you have to pretend you have faith, even if you don't believe. I'm always telling Don Marcelo, it's fine for priests to eat their fill, drink the best wine, even fornicate. But they have to make an effort to believe, because people need faith. Here nobody believes in anything. That's the problem. It's all in Unamuno, yes sirree!'

He attracted Rumbo's attention. Without words, using a series of gestures the other man interpreted with a nod. Shortly afterwards the barman placed a bottle of Johnnie Walker on the table.

'Without taxes! It came by sea, as saints used to in Galicia.'

'You'll have a lot of stories to tell, Mariscal,' said the doctor. 'Some magnificent, diabolical memoirs!'

Mariscal rang the ice in his glass. Took a sip, which he savoured.

'Sincerity's not good for business. As you well know, I spent some time in the seminary. There's lots of gossip, lots of rumours. Spineless stuff! Rubbish, most of it. But today's a good day for confessing. Once the director of the seminary called me to one side and asked if I really had a vocation. I told him of course I did. But how much of a vocation, he wanted to know. I replied, a lot. Yes, but how much? And that's when I told him I wanted to be pope. He turned pale as wax. As if I'd uttered the most terrible thing.'

'So you didn't say you wanted to be God?' asked Dr Fonseca ironically.

'No. That's a legend. Though it's true that a young lad from Nazareth tried it and managed it. To become God.' He drank a second sip. Clicked his tongue. 'Had I told you that before? Oh, what a shame! That's the trouble with us ancients.'

'Another drink?' asked Rumbo.

The two of them had been alone for some time. Without talking. From the back of the bar came the sound of urgent voices, shots and the screeching of cars and trains. On the television, Brinco was watching *The Fugitive*.

'What does a tiger care about one more stripe?'

Sira came out of the kitchen. In time to encounter her husband, who was returning with the supplies. Another bottle of Johnnie Walker.

'Where are you off to? That's enough for today!'

Mariscal jumped up on hearing her thundering voice. But when he tried to move, he stumbled.

'A coffee!' he exclaimed, stretching his sense of comedy. 'How would sir like his coffee, with or without brandy? Without coffee!'

The joke was addressed to Sira, but she ignored him.

'Never mind,' he mumbled, heading for the exit. 'Open the door, it's not going to fit!'

'I'll take him,' said Rumbo.

Mariscal turned around and pointed at the barman. 'No you won't! Do you want us both to be killed, Simca 1000? I'll get a breath of fresh air. The sea has a cure for everything.'

'You can sleep here if you like,' said Sira. 'The inn is yours.'

Now Mariscal was the one who felt tense. Bad-tempered. 'No way! Mariscal always spends the night in his own home.'

'Go with him!' said Sira to Brinco.

The boy rose mechanically to his feet without saying a word, as if this was the outcome he'd been expecting. Went behind the bar and came back with a torch.

'Good idea,' said Mariscal. 'Let's ride out the storm!'

Brinco went ahead, walking uneasily, moving the torch up and down, from side to side, deliberately, like a machete. Behind him, Mariscal hummed. Puffed and panted. Hummed. Paused to catch his breath.

'It's a bit cold,' he murmured.

When they reached the new wharf, near the centre of town, Brinco directed the torch towards the water. At the mouth of the sewer, which led directly into the sea, was a horde of mullet. A nervous crowd of intertwined bodies in the muck.

A section of the marine golem twisted and turned in the glare of the torch. Mariscal peered over. 'Those gluttons will eat anything, even the light!'

At this point he tripped on the edge of a stone and slipped

a little, stumbling right on the edge of the wharf. He managed very carefully to sit down on a bollard. Brinco was right behind him. Mariscal realised the boy hadn't moved a muscle. As if the accident had never happened.

The beam of the torch ran over the voracious cluster of fish in the sewage.

'Yes, they'll eat the light,' said Mariscal. 'Look at them chewing!'

He let himself go, leaned forward, as if the fall was inevitable. But just then Brinco grabbed hold of him and pulled him back on to firm ground.

II Mute Silence

17

The back room of the Ultramar is filled with the impatience that comes with the end of a hand. The players of *mus* and *tute* make up for the blazoned silence of the cards with sharp voices and authoritative raps of their knuckles on the tables. In the games of dominoes, by contrast, it is the discharge of matter that can be heard, tokens on marble, in an ascending scale of blasts excited by the advance of the victorious combination. The middle of the room is occupied by a billiard table ignored by everyone except for the trails of cigar smoke that have gathered in a storm beneath the central lamp.

At Mariscal's table there sounds the percussion of dominoes. He likes to adorn suspense. Hold the piece in the air for a moment, its value hidden from sight, before revealing the enigma with a thwack that, on triumphant occasions, is followed by outbursts of strange historical consequences. 'Tremble, Toledo! *Carthago delenda est.*'

Mariscal is on the verge of playing, but seems distracted. As almost always, he's wearing his white gloves, which act as a shade whenever the piece is bad. He looks up at the other end of the room, above the door. There, on a ledge, is a desiccated bird in a glass case. A little owl. Its eyes shine with an electric gleam. Two illuminated lights. Inverno follows his boss's gaze.

'Looks like the owl's not going to sleep tonight.'

'Those bastards are behind schedule,' replies Mariscal.

'Do you think we've an informer, boss?'

'No, what we've got is a new bedbug. That sergeant knows very well what he has to do. But tomorrow he'll up the stakes, you'll see. Tell us there's another mouth that needs feeding.'

He allows his thoughts to be heard, that constant, subordinated rumour. 'Though it comes from filthy hands, money always smells of roses,' etc., etc. He gazes at the token's symmetry. A double three.

'And we'll have no choice but to pay! That's the way the world works, Inverno. There's no professionalism any more.'

Brinco and Chelín's mission is to prevent any intruders from entering the back room, which is separated from the bar by two steps and some swing doors. What they do, in effect, is act as sitting mummies. If anyone approaches, even if what they want is to play billiards, though not a sound of this game can be heard, however ignorant or foreign they may be, a simple sideways glance from Brinco, of the kind that says *go jerk off a dead man*, is usually more than dissuasive.

So they concentrate their attention on the sergeant and the man with him. There is a third, Haroldo Grimaldo – Micho – a veteran inspector who sometimes drops into the Ultramar. Often he drops in the literal sense.

'He's half pissed already,' says Brinco. 'The only thing that saves him is his suspicion. He can see the demijohn before it's reached him. He's the one who's clairvoyant, not you.'

Víctor is talking about Grimaldo, but his gaze is fixed on Leda, who sometimes helps out as a waitress. With her slender body. Her blazing long hair. Black pirate trousers. Tight-fitting white T-shirt. She's good at her job, thinks Brinco, because she knows how to be with people. How to be and not to be. She doesn't dole out sugar to horses.

In ceremonial style, Chelín gets out his pendulum. While he holds it in front of himself, it doesn't move. He guides it gently towards Brinco, who's sitting next to him, on the steps to the back room. The pendulum begins to swing. It accelerates when the centre of gravity is located above Brinco's groin.

'Brinco, you're on fire!'

The other man grabs his wrist. The pendulum swings even faster.

'It's your pulse, you idiot!'

'Sure, the throbbing of your dicky bird.'

Chelín seeks out Leda with his gaze. He knows where the magnetic pole is situated. She really is worth committing a crime for. She and Brinco have been living as a couple for some time. Soon after they got together, they had a child. And here they are. Who'd have said it of Víctor, the greatest pilot in Noitía, a real wild card, that he'd stick to a single nest. Contrary to expectations, she hadn't been just another lobster in the pot, another prawn in the cocktail, another woman for hire.

'You like her, don't you? You've always liked her.'

It's Brinco who says this suddenly to Chelín. He remains silent. Like a fool. The pendulum in the air, now still.

'Why don't you go and measure her battery with that bullet of yours?' says Brinco.

In other circumstances, Chelín would stay where he is. He's used to the fact that Brinco's thoughts, words and deeds don't always match. You have to read between the lines. The moments when he is nice are the most perilous. They're like little gifts before he takes off. There are other moments when he's delirious, not working. Right now Chelín decides to take him at his word and play along. The game with the pendulum. He gets up. Goes over to Leda. Holds the pendulum in front of her breasts. The bullet starts swaying madly.

'Leda, look how you put it into orbit,' gasps Chelín. 'You're a universal dynamo.'

'It's your pulse,' she replies. 'I can hear your heart. The beating of a mouse.'

Brinco comes over. Chelín doesn't know whether he's smiling or threatening. His mouth has that thick-lipped scar, which never really healed. Because of where he's looking, in the end Chelín comes to the conclusion, with some relief, that this has nothing to do with him.

'Give that to me!' says Brinco, taking the pendulum out of his hands.

Chelín quickly tries to work out the direction of his gaze. There's not much point in him surveying the pair of guards. They're dressed in plain clothes, or as Mariscal would say, their plain clothes are their uniform. One of them is an old acquaintance, Sergeant Montes. They should have left long ago, but they're still here. It's their job to guard the guards. So what's he doing?

Brinco stares arrogantly at the guards. Raises the pendulum. The bullet on the end of a chain. They pretend not to notice. The sergeant makes out he's reading the newspaper, but he's spent all afternoon on the same page. His colleague sips a soft drink rather too slowly. 'Coca-Colo', Brinco calls him.

'Víctor! What's going on?'

Brinco turns around. Rumbo is calling him from the bar. There's something in his codified look.

'Nothing. Nothing's going on.'

Brinco holds the pendulum in front of his eyes and lets it take him in search of Leda.

Eventually the sergeant attracts Leda's attention with a click and gesture of his fingers and asks how much they owe. She looks at Rumbo inquisitively. He gives Montes a clear answer. Without words. The cross he makes with his hands says, 'It's on the house. Everything's paid. Till next time.'

Once the guards have left the premises, the barman presses a switch under the counter. In the back room, the little owl's eyes finally go out. A sign, the switching on and off of the lights, that is repeated three times. Until the eyes are extinguished.

'Finally! Let's get moving. Inverno, Carburo, let's conquer the West!'

Mariscal heads towards the billiard table and grabs the cue. Everyone else has suspended their game. The cards and pieces, which seconds earlier were hooting and cawing like carriers of destiny, have lost their purpose and are abandoned haphazardly.

'Sorry, gentlemen, but night has fallen,' begins Mariscal. 'If anyone has domestic obligations, well . . . I don't want anyone's wife to be annoyed with me. No one? Good. This could be a great day for all of us. For . . . the Society.'

Mariscal surveys the billiard table as if he's just discovered *terra incognita*.

'You all know what a *mamma* is, now, don't you?'

He is clearly bursting at the seams. With a message for the world.

'Always thinking about one thing . . . A woman takes her child to the doctor's and the doctor enquires, "How's it going? Is the baby sucking well?" And the mother replies, "Very well, Doctor! Just like an adult."'

This is followed by the first round of nods and laughter.

'Talking of sucking people dry, we have a new lawyer. A brilliant guy, who should be around here somewhere. Try and avoid him. You all know priests and lawyers are not allowed on board.'

Their looks seek out Óscar Mendoza and quickly find him

on account of the spotless suit and refined bearing which contrast with the sheepskin coats and leather jackets.

'Humour's good for business. There's lots of bitterness and what money wants is joy. Money's like people!'

He turns his attention back to the billiard table. Changes expression. He has a collection of faces, which he puts to good use. Thoughtful. Serious.

'Go on then, Carburo!'

To everyone's surprise, Carburo pulls back the green felt from one corner and quickly rolls it up to reveal a large map of Europe. Maritime coordinates in the Mediterranean and Atlantic are marked with a red cross where a second assistant, Inverno, deposits billiard balls.

Mariscal follows the operation carefully, with an enigmatic half-smile, and when his subordinate has finished, he uses the cue as a pointer, gently stroking the balls as he reveals the crux of his discourse.

'Gentlemen, look. There are twenty-five *mammas* loaded with tobacco along the coasts of Europe. Most are in the Mediterranean. Near Greece, Italy, Sicily and in those parts. There are also several in the Adriatic, next to the communist countries. They enjoy a bit of vice just as much as we do!'

He pauses for effect, remaining thoughtful and serious while the others laugh at his joke. Then he makes another movement with the cue, which is like wielding a baton. And heads westwards in the middle of absolute silence.

'Where are we?'

He suddenly bangs the table with the cue.

'Right here! North-west quarter west. *Sensu stricto.*'

Everyone gazes at their home. The surprise that comes from viewing where you live from the outside.

'If we head further south, just a little bit, we come to the part that interests us. A *mamma*. Our very own *mamma*. Right here, very close, in northern Portugal. Of course it's not our *mamma* in the sense of ownership. We've been suckling until recently on Delmiro Oliveira's. Now Mr Oliveira is a man with a sense of humour. I said to him, "Listen, Delmiro, do you know what a Galician hates most of all?" And he replied, "No, I don't." And I said, "What a Galician hates most of all is being subservient to someone from Portugal."'

The border joke is accompanied by smiles. But they remain silent. Watchful.

'You see? He laughed as well. Because he's a skilled businessman. And has a sense of humour. He understood. And said, "I don't have servants, Mariscal. I have partners. What's more," he continued, "I've no desire to be a Midas, a shit who feeds on other people's leftovers." Now that Delmiro guy is smart.'

Mariscal lifts his head with satisfaction and surveys the room.

'What made Delmiro Oliveira understand? What made them understand in Antwerp and Switzerland? They understood that we have something. We have the best arguments for business. An amazing, endless coastline full of nooks and crannies. A secret sea which keeps us safe. And we're the closest to the mother port, to the source. So we've got everything. Coast, depots, boats, men. And most important of all, we've got balls!'

He gestures to quieten the jovial uproar. Addresses a corner of the room, where someone sits on the margins, split by a diagonal line dividing light from shade.

'*È vero o non è vero, Tonino?*'

'It's true, boss. And no mistake.'

18

Fins had his eyes closed. When you close your eyes, beware of what might open. He took a deep breath, let it go slowly, like a mouth of wind. He heard a snort that attracted his attention. Aroused him from his absence. A herd of horses was grazing on the eastern slope of the mirador, where the morning sun lazily disentangled the strips of mist. The stallion's gaze, pricked ears, defensive teeth, warning neigh, reminded him he was a nuisance. A stranger, a poacher, in his own land.

On top of the mountain named Curota, part of the Barbanza range, were large rocks with a wish to be altars. The highest one was reached by a flight of steps carved out of the stone. Fins climbed them.

Before his eyes stretched the broadest maritime view in the whole of Galicia. He looked south, had the impression he could make out the earth's curve. It was the best place to see the estuary, which appeared as a vast stage. A marine womb set in earth. Across each other's wake moved very different kinds of seafaring vessels. Crane boats headed in the direction of palafittic floating structures, the large estates that were the mussel platforms.

Fins glanced now to his right. There, in the west, was the open, the Atlantic Ocean. An infinite, restless monotony of hoarse mercury in the process of meltdown shielded the enigma. Each ripple or blade of light seemed to release the bud of a seabird. Their screeches grew louder, as when they had good or bad news to tell. A burgeoning shoal, a storm. The sky appeared clear, but it wasn't an enthusiastic clarity.

Behind the line of the horizon, no one knows how the dead water will awake.

The sound of an engine came up the road. Fins hid behind the rocks.

The person driving didn't hesitate. He turned, followed the other tracks, parked the Mercedes-Benz with whitewall tyres in the large expanse of the first mirador.

The Old Man had got up early. Been forced to take a roundabout route. Follow the line of the estuary. This wasn't a run-of-the-mill appointment. He never made a phone call in person. He used carrier pigeons, people he could trust. So this wasn't an ordinary assignation. The fish he'd been sold wasn't rotten. Fins climbed down through the gorse, sought out a good position. Felt the camera inside his jacket, stroked the Nikon F as he'd seen a hunter stroke his ferret when he was a child. Mariscal stood with his back to him. There was no mistaking the white linen suit, the panama hat and steel-tipped cane. Facing the other way, next to the stone bust of Ramón María del Valle-Inclán, his bearing was sculptural.

Time passed and both spy and target began to grow impatient. Mariscal glanced at his pocket watch twice, but not as often as he glanced at the sky in the west. There where you could see the first line of the Azores front. A logging truck slowly ground its way uphill. Mariscal followed it out of the corner of his eye until it disappeared around the corner, in the direction of the mountain.

Fins hadn't lost hope. All his life he'd been trained to deal with the unexpected. There was the sound of heavy machinery.

A storm always starts by sending in the air force. Mariscal glanced at his watch a third time. The way he placed it in the pocket of his waistcoat, it was his ferret. He surveyed the surrounding area with suspicion. The writer's stone bust as well. Banged the base of the plinth with his cane to shake off any mud. Went into reverse and then returned the way he'd come.

Fins patted his camera affectionately.

A day is a day.

Someone had gone and sold the same fish twice.

19

'Mother. Can you hear me, mother? It's me, Fins!'

She eyed him again in surprise. 'Fins? There was a party. My son will be called Emilio. Milucho. Lucho.'

'It's a good name, isn't it, mother? I'm going to work there, in Noitía.'

Again that surprise in Amparo's tone of voice. 'Noitía, Noitía . . . I spent an afternoon in Noitía, buying thread. It was hot, very hot. The whole place was burning from the inside out, like a log. And I got caught in a storm.'

They fell silent. Whenever the word 'storm' was mentioned, the other words waited a bit.

'What are you going to work as?'

'As a secret agent,' he said in order to see her reaction.

She did what Fins least expected. She burst out laughing. 'A secret agent? There'll be lots of those!'

Fins now, for her, was the memory of an outing. Nothing more. Lucho Malpica, a child who was yet to be born. And Noitía, a nightmarish place, a place she'd gone to one day to buy thread and been attacked by a storm. She was behind him, calm, unconcerned, with her cushion, teaching her carer the secret art of making lace. He stood staring at the sea through a large window which let in the combined sound of the waves' hiss and the seagulls' scream. He'd have loved to draw the curtain. Cover that vision. He couldn't understand people who found gazing at the sea restful. For him it was deeply disturbing. He couldn't bear to be alone with the sea for more than five minutes. And it seemed the feeling was mutual. He was sure its mood changed and it grew angry whenever he stood looking at it.

Diving was something else. When you were inside the sea, that was different. The only way to understand the sea was by getting wet. Surveying the underwater forests of kelp, sea lettuce, thongweed, bladderwrack, toothed wrack, knotted wrack, sea fans, sugar kelp, purple seaweed such as carrageen or Irish moss. Sailing, on the surface, he got seasick, felt as if he was dying. He sneezed, spat, drawled, coughed up his lungs, liver, prefixes, saliva, interjections, onomatopoeias, phlegm, tubercles, roots, bile, the inaccessible; the worst thing was throwing up what came after the void, after air, all of it yellow, the sky, sea, skin, the back of the eyes, the soul. Except when he was rowing. If he was rowing, and the more energy he put into it the better, with his back towards his destination, there was a temporary suspension of the disease. But he had to make sure he kept going.

He closed the window of the room and all he could hear was the unmistakable knocking of the boxwood needles. They were in a home for old people and not such old people with Alzheimer's. Amparo's illness was something else. She was convinced she could remember everything.

'Poor things! They sometimes forget their own names. I'm the one who has to remind them.'

She tapped her forehead with her index and middle fingers. 'It's all in here!'

Next to Amparo was her carer, a young and kind girl.

'Her hands get more and more agile,' she said. 'Look at them. It's as if the skin is smoother and her hands move more quickly. Good hands for making lace, aren't they, Amparo? And who's this little marvel for?'

Amparo Malpica stared through the large window with melancholy.

'It's for my son. For when he's born.'

The neuropsychiatrist had said, 'Her mind has suppressed a time that hurts her. Her illness is a property. The property of erasing a period of her life. Or at least erasing it as an explicit memory. Something we call retrograde amnesia.' The period she'd kept alive was precisely her experience as a girl, before she left Uz and went to live with Lucho in the seaside house in A de Meus. Fins knew the dynamite had exploded not only on the boat. His mother, in her own way, had put an end to a life that included him. But seeing her there, physically well, with her agile fingers, that fertile gaze, dispossessed of the fears that used to hold sway over her, knowing her name, smiling at anyone passing by, he couldn't help feeling annoyed.

'So what you're saying is she forgets what she wants to forget?' he asked reproachfully.

Talking to Dr Facal, he had the impression that he was before the sea and the sea was stronger than him.

'No. Memory is often painful. She's gone past the limit of pain. In order to survive, her mind has rejected the bit that's hurting her. Memory has these strategies. She could have chosen a different path. But she's chosen this one. We'll never fully understand why.'

'Is it reversible?'

The doctor took her time. In Fins' experience, he knew that if the answer was positive, he'd have been told it already.

'The truth isn't always pleasant,' she said eventually.

And this was the truest thing he'd hear in a long time.

20

'Isn't that the son of Malpica, the one who died using dynamite?'

They gazed from the sea. Used to seeing from the outside in. From west to east. From darkness to dawn. From mist to morning. At varying depths. Several of them half submerged, the water around their waists. They moved like amphibians, with effective slowness, overcoming hydraulic resistance with their home-made diving suits of waterproof clothing over wool, their whole bodies like pistons plunging down, digging, scratching, harvesting the sea with ancient implements, long-handled hoes, rakes, forks. Their heads covered in an array of scarves and hats.

These women had been his world. They'd all passed through it. Guadalupe, Amparo, Sira, Adela, Belvís' mother, Chelín's mother, even Leda, with their buckets full of cockles and sacks of clams.

'It is. I heard he studied to become a policeman.'

'Do you have to study for that?'

'It all depends ... Not if you want to walk around with a truncheon in your hand, like your husband.'

'That's right, woman!' The gatherer of shellfish gestured with the rake between her legs. 'I bet you wish your husband had a truncheon like mine!'

They all burst out laughing.

'Go wash out your mouth!'

'Leda . . . she's a clever one.'

The shellfish harvesters resumed their work. In search of molluscs, their bodies transformed themselves into strange, prehistoric monsters.

'They say he's going to be an inspector, a secret investigator.'

'It can't be that secret if you know all about it!'

'That's what I heard. Doesn't bother me! He can be an astronaut for all I care.'

'Oooh, an astronaut would be nice!'

The women's voices and laughter combined at that hour with the sea's phonemes, the screeching and splashing, greedy warnings of vigilant birds. Fins couldn't help himself. He took a photograph. Just one. And withdrew like a poacher.

In front of the house in A de Meus, the hand on the door, calling outwards. Inside what gave him the warmest welcome was the oilskin tablecloth, on which stood an abandoned bottle, with a trail of wine like a tidemark. At dusk Fins wandered along the coastal road. Stopped at Chafariz Cross, where he used to wait for the bus. Stuck his hands in his trouser pockets. A normal man should always have some spare change. He hesitated. He had a good excuse for staying where he was. But by the time he realised, his feet had already transported him to the door of the bar. He could hear the hustle and bustle of a Friday night.

Without touching the door handle, he moved to one side and peered in. The luminous novelties of the Rock-Ola and game machines.

Behind the glass, in that large belljar, memory fermented.

Life twisted and turned to the sound of music. With him on the outside.

Rumbo was filling glasses on a tray placed on the counter.

A little further down, on the other side of the counter, Leda and Víctor. He was sitting on a tall stool with a glass in his hand, looking serious. She was standing up, playing with her finger at curling the taciturn man's hair. At that point the mocking, seductive gesture was the centre of the world. A gesture he recognised, which said, 'Where are you?'

Leda turned to heed Rumbo's call. Fins could see her face to face. The pottery of time had improved any memory. He was afraid he might be seen, he who was an expert in angles of shade. A specialist in shade. He could measure the textile thickness of shadows. There were shadows of satin, wool, cotton, nylon, polyester, velvet. Transparent. Waterproof. But when he peeped in again, she had her back to him, with the tray in her hand. From the eye of the catafalque, life became painful again. People were coming. He ran away from their intrusive radiance.

21

Well, look who's coming. Look who's just come in. I'm not surprised the bats are bothered. They've been hanging there for months, chewing on the shade, and now they've woken. Hear, I don't think they have any problem hearing, and anyway Malpica has forgotten where to put his feet. Who'd have thought he'd end up looking so ugly? He knocks against all the geographical features. We're all right. I'm a local. My nest is made. The blind mannequin and the one-armed skeleton no longer surprise me. Or the desiccated crane. How well they did those eyes. Those little dots that look everywhere at once. Wherever I am, they can see me. They're watching out for me. I found my place. My hide-away. Even the pendulum has calmed down. And in this little corner, this screened cubbyhole with its slats of disarranged books, there's a scent of coves, as if the sea itself came up here one night, to the map of wood, and left all these cracks and beads. The box with its glass lid and sign that says 'Malacology', whoever thought of that name, full of all kinds of shells and periwinkles, which I took out of the grid and put somewhere else. There were also collections of butterflies, beetles and spiders imported from America, some of them as big as your fist. I have respect for spiders. I once squashed one, a little one, on my best shirt. It was a white shirt and the bug kept climbing up, so in the end I squashed it. Never squash a spider on your shirt. You wouldn't believe the amount of blood a bug like that can hold. A whole life's worth. The same as a hit. The gentle pulling of the piston once you've found the vein. The colour of blood, the initial colour, can handle everything. The same with the amber liquid. And then you pump blood of your own blood. A blood pump. In three movements. I like to pump in three movements.

The point is, several years ago, when I was more hung up than ever, they saved my life. I gathered and sold the zoological troop, the ranked creepy-crawlies, spiders, silver-plated beetles, American butterflies. I said to the guy, 'I've brought you the whole of Genesis, this lot is worth a fortune.' So he went and gave me a ball of smack, 'Here's your globe, so you can stuff it up your arm.' That's why there are species, so I can get a fix. But not the collection of malacology. He didn't want to see it. It must have been because of the name. Or because we're sick of shells around here. Not me. I get genuinely sentimental whenever I set eyes on anything remotely shelly. Like the conch of a hermit. Now that's what I call architecture. That is art. Like sea urchins. That is beauty, their spines. If I was standing face to face with one of those famous artists, I'd stick a sea urchin in his hands and say, 'Go on then, do it, if you've got the balls!' There has to be a mysterious mystery for such symmetries to grow in the sea. Now they're uninhabited, the crabs have gone to hell, but the shells are good company, they adorn the ruins on this side of the School of Indians. The hermit crabs will be hiding behind some geographical feature, I suppose. I'm not quite sure what part of the world I'm in. It feels like the Antarctic on account of the cold. But everything went well. Everything was going well. The spoon secure, stuck between two volumes of *Civilisation*. Don Pelegrín Casabó y Pagés. Chronicles can be extremely useful. Thank God for *Civilisation*. At the height of his work, my hands are free to warm the smack in the water. To see the amber colour of smelting. And so on until you pump the geographical feature in three movements.

I didn't forget that bit about the geographical features. 'The eagle now is hunting flies. Tell me, Balboa, the names of some geographical features.' It's funny what stays and what doesn't. That teacher, Lame, Exile, always used to say, 'We are what we remember.' What do I know? We are what we remember. We are what we forget. Whenever I forget something, I stick my tongue where my tooth is missing. Where all the things I forget go. I've a hiding place there that is a bottomless well. Exile also said, 'Nothing is heavy for someone with wings. You have wings, don't you?' Of course I have wings, Don Basilio. Like Belvís. He wasn't a bad guy, Don Basilio, though he looked tired of children and was always playing around in the clouds or out gathering words. That's what he was like, always on the trail of other sayings, in the same way we used to search for grapes left over from the harvest. When he came down, he did so very carefully. One day he asked what we wanted to be when we were older, and I went and said, 'A smuggler!' He replied, 'Better to say "entrepreneur", child. "Entrepreneur"!'

That catechist with the cropped white hair told us we all had an angel. A guardian angel, we all knew that. But she gave details. She wasn't fooling around. There were angels whose task was to watch over and care for God's throne, organise the celestial rehearsals. I could understand that. It all seemed reasonable enough. God's not going to keep tabs on everything, on whether they move his chair this way or that, what time the sun is going to rise, whether there's a flood over here and a drought over there. And then there are the guardian angels, those who side with us, with the flock we are. I really liked the explanation about why they aren't visible, why they don't have a shadow, so to speak. Because they're a profession, not matter. They come and go, do their work, this is good, that isn't, but they don't inspect you, don't pop the bill in the post or pester you. They work and let others work without getting in the way. If it wasn't like that, it would hardly be life. For you or for them. 'Where you going?' 'I dunno, for a walk.' 'What you using that for?' 'I like it.' 'It ain't good, you know it ain't good.' 'If I like it, it can be good, so stop bugging me.' 'What you want a weapon for?' 'What weapon?' 'That pipe.' 'What pipe?' Blasted angel, digging around where he's not wanted, his feathers on fire. But on the other hand, you know your Guardian A. is there for you, to give you a message and bugger off. That's what I would call a transparent profession. Then we'll get the Last Judgement. Sounds reasonable enough. 'Proceedings were instituted, here you have the report on so-and-so.' 'Mr Xosé Luís Balboa, also known as Chelín, we understand from your Guardian Angel that you were in possession of a firearm. What was it for?' 'For lining dogs up against the wall, Mr St Michael.' 'Very well, let us proceed to weigh your soul.' At which point St Michael gets out the scales for weighing human souls, which are remarkably like the scales used by a refined dealer who supplied me in a villa on the outskirts of Coruña. Shame that catechist never came back. That girl I met once in the disco Xornes. With the cropped hair. She looked younger than she really was. Had a man's hoarse voice. She must have been an angel. Because there's a third class of angels, or so I understand. Errant angels like her. For whom sky and earth are closed.

And in he comes, Ugly Mug, digging around. I'd just got my fix, the flash had gone by and I was coming down slowly. I was back in the Antarctic, next to Malacology, and thinking of giving Don Pelegrín a go. You can't read very well in the semi-darkness of the Antarctic, but I've read plenty of saints in here. I've a soft spot for Lord Byron. You what? Lord Byron contemplating the freedom of Greece. And in he comes, stepping on the geographical features. Sticking his nose in where it's not wanted. Both matter and profession. He could be an eagle, I suppose. While he's up north, he won't spot me. All the same, I'd better put the tools in the shed of *Civilisation*, stay still as the crane, between the planks of wood. He'll be reminiscing about Johnnie Walker. He sits down at the teacher's desk. Pokes around inside the typewriter. Removes bits of fallen tiles. Blows away the fluff and dust. Pulls a handkerchief out of his pocket. Wipes the keys, bars, carriage, platen. Starts typing with his eyes closed. Mission nostalgia, Malpica!

O my godmother! You never know where to expect her next! Be amazed, blind mannequin. Be amazed, one-armed skeleton. Well, blow me down. Be amazed, Mr Crane. Be amazed, Mr Chelín. Because who should enter the stage but Nine Moons! Earth, swallow me up. No, Leda, you shouldn't be here. What's she doing in Operation Nostalgia? A century, a millennium, has gone by. Franco snuffed it years ago. Some weirdo went and shot John Lennon. Leda's working in the Ultramar. She has a son with Brinco. And Brinco, well, he's the number one. When Brinco's involved, everything goes swimmingly. He's the best pilot in the whole estuary. The best pilot in the world. There's not a submarine will catch him. He's got himself an iron angel, a fearless guardian. The women are crazy about him. What you doing here, girl?

Mr Nosy starts typing without paper. Reads aloud what he's typing.

'All is mute silense . . .'

'You see? Was I right or not?' says Leda. 'Didn't I tell you she wrote "silense" with an "s"? And you kept laughing, saying how would Rosalía de Castro write "silense" with an "s"?'

'You were right. She could hear. "Silense" is more silent when it's written like that,' remarks Fins. The hole in the roof has grown bigger and the areas of shade on the map are smaller. 'You can see better now. Your nails are painted black. You're in the ocean.'

'Like always. In the middle of the fucking ocean. Where letters never arrive. Just condolences. It was kind of you to write whenever someone died. My dad, the schoolteacher, the doctor. The condolences looked as if they'd come straight out of a book of correspondence.'

'I remembered you, everything here, more than you can imagine.'

'Every day, at all hours, right? I could feel some kind of Morse. Keys from the beyond. Of course you were learning how to touch-type. That must have taken a while.'

Fins gets up and heads towards her. Leda retreats until she's leaning against the teacher's desk, back in the shadows. As he approaches, she spits on the ground, in the sea, between the two of them. He remains still, quiet.

'Well, I didn't. I learned how to forget. Every hour of every day. I'm an expert at forgetting.'

'To tell the truth, I thought a lot about myself. My life. And time went by.'

'The boy with the absences!'

'That's in the past. I'm better now. Far too present.'

'I have a son,' she says with growing confidence. 'A son by Víctor.'

Yes, he knows.

'What do you want? Me to talk about Brinco? About Rumbo? The Old Man's business? The Ultramar's secrets?'

She realises her own cocky tongue has lost control of its traction. She's about to say something concerning dynamite. But the word gets stuck. Goes back. Like the mouse scurrying across the ocean, through the rubble.

'Do you know why I'm here, Fins Malpica? I have a message for you. I never want to see you again. Don't call me, don't talk to me, don't even look at me. Understand?'

'I'm not going to ask you for anything, Leda,' replies Fins. 'Or give you anything. Even if you ask, I've nothing left to give.'

They've gone now. What a conversation! Straight out of some soap. But it moved me. It really did. I was feeling so well, my warm body in the cold of the Antarctic, a tingling in my feet, thinking about the art of sea urchins and hermit crabs. My God, there was pain in both of them. I could see them as children playing on the beach the day they found the mannequin and carried it here, to the School of Indians. The jokes they had to put up with that day. And now I stay in my dark corner, huddled up, stiff with cold, staring at the great couple, the blind manne-quin and the one-armed skeleton. I wonder what the dealer would give for them. A lump of hash. A globe of smack. Enough for two shots at least. He wouldn't even open the door, the bastard. They're obviously priceless.

Mariscal had a habit of rising with the sun. Having gone around various miradors, a duty he liked to fulfil with proud punctuality, in the mornings he would sit by the window to read the news-papers. He'd sometimes stop to do the crossword. Like today. He didn't turn around, but heard the blast that opened the door and noisily cleared a way between stools and chairs before coming to an abrupt halt beside him. He'd nearly completed the cross-word. He made it obvious he was in some doubt by repeatedly tapping the biro. He could hear a hum, the electric field of Brinco Furioso.

'Where is Leda?'

'Give me a hand here, will you? "Part of the chequebook that is left once the cheque has been removed."'

'Fuck, Mariscal.'

'F-U-C-K. No, it's not "fuck".'

'I don't give a damn if he has a badge. I'm going to eat him up and vomit him off the bridge.'

Mariscal puffed on his Havana cigar and chewed, ground down the smoke. When he exhaled, the smoke was thick and stuck to the word, which appeared in the squares.

'S-T-U-B. Now that's it.'

He turned his head and glanced at the crazed lover.

'Listen, Víctor Rumbo. I don't like being shouted at from above and certainly not from behind.'

Brinco sat down opposite him. With a furrowed brow, but subdued gaze.

'I sent her to see Malpica. To find out what the bastard wants. We need information. Information, Brinco!'

22

The old light that spilled from the fluorescent strips still slid down the wall to illuminate the name of the dance hall and cinema Paris-Noitía. It could be spotted from the beach, at least by Fins Malpica. In the same way he could hear Sira's voice, that refrain, 'I'm not going, I'm not going', which strangely made it easier to walk. 'The prettiest love can go by, I'm not going, I'm not going.' When, on a Sunday evening, she was persuaded to sing, things in the estuary already had their shadowy side. This was something Fins remembered, seeing his shadow projected on the shore. The eager progression of shadows towards the dance hall.

'I'm not going, I'm not going.'

The cinema had closed some time before. And the dance hall opened only rarely to host some prearranged party. A footprint in the sand, 'I'm not going', another, 'I'm not going'. He was far away, but inside he could see and hear. Memory had the intensity of an absence. He couldn't tell anybody. He'd been back in Noitía for almost a year and the *petit mal* had returned several months earlier. The episodes were much more spaced out. But he could see them coming. They passed like intermittences. Blinks. The opening and closing of a window. He had a name for these absences. The Argonaut's void. Because it was the *petit mal*, yes. But it was his *petit mal*.

Shortly after he left, the absences had disappeared. He thought the inconvenience would never reappear. And to begin with, when he returned, he didn't have any short circuits. He could have said his mind went before him. Functioned well. He knew he had a long way to go, but he was starting to possess threads to weave with.

So the *petit mal* wasn't exactly an illness. After a single absence, in an outburst of humour, he decided to make it a property. A secret belonging.

He stopped hearing the song, seeing the spectre of letters in the dance hall. From where he was, in the ruins of the salting factory, Fins could see San Telmo wharf. It was illuminated by a few street lamps. He could see people moving, but not distinguish them all clearly. Study their shadows. That was his trade.

At the end of the dyke, where there was a small lighthouse, stood two men. He could recognise them from a distance. One was unmistakable, with his hat and steel-tipped cane, moving in and out of the circles of light. When he was in a circle, Fins could see the white of his gloves and the tips of his shoes. It looked as if he was about to start tap-dancing. This was Mariscal. His eternal bodyguard, Carburo the giant, stood with his arms crossed, surveying everything, moving his head in time to the lighthouse beacon.

Brinco came marching down the new dyke. He was wearing a black leather jacket that turned into patent leather whenever it passed under one of the lamps. Behind him, in similar clothes, but with more zips and metal reinforcements, came Chelín, his lackey.

On several shallow-water boats preparations were under way to go out fishing. The sailors were laying out the tackle.

'Hey, Brinco!' shouted one of the younger sailors.

Víctor Rumbo carried on his way, but not without depositing a confidential greeting: 'Everything OK?'

'Doing what we can, Brinco.' And then, to his companion, 'See? That was Brinco.'

'You sure?'

'Of course I am! We played football together. Look. The other's Chelín. Tito Balboa. A very fine goalie!'

'Wasn't he an addict?'

'That guy always walked on the edge. For better and for worse.'

In his hiding place, however much the sea amplified their voices, Fins couldn't make out their conversation. But he could hear the admiring salutations Víctor Rumbo received.

'See you, Brinco!'

'See you, champ!'

'You sent for me?'

Mariscal responded with a cough, a kind of affirmative growl. Then cleared his throat. 'It's about time you were a little less formal, Víctor.'

'Yes, boss,' said Brinco as if he hadn't heard.

The Old Man gazed at the waters, which appeared calm but grumbled discontentedly against the dyke. 'All the best stuff comes from the sea! All of it.'

'Without the need for a single shovelful of manure!'

'Have I told you that before?'

'Yes, boss.'

'That's the trouble with us ancients. We're in the habit of repeating ourselves.'

Mariscal scratched his throat again. Stared at Víctor,

adopting a more intimate tone of voice. 'You're the best pilot, Brinco!'

'So they tell me . . .'

'No, you are!'

Mariscal gestured to Carburo, who pulled a torch out of his pocket, switched it on and pointed it at the sea, creating Morse-like signals. They soon heard the sound of a motorboat that must have been waiting in the wings. Not a normal kind of boat. The roar of its horsepower overwhelmed the night.

'Well, the best pilot deserves a bonus, an incentive!'

No such vessel had ever been seen in Noitía before. A speed-boat of this length, its power increased by multiple engines on the stern. Inverno steered it towards the dyke.

'How's that barge then, Inverno?'

The subaltern was wildly enthusiastic.

'It's not a speedboat, boss. It's a frigate! A flagship! We could cross the Atlantic in this!'

'It has enough horsepower to travel around the world,' boasted Mariscal. And then to Brinco, 'What do you think?'

'I'm checking out the horsepower.'

'The flagship's yours!' said Mariscal. 'And there's no need to worry about the paperwork.' He was overseeing delivery. 'The boat's in your mother's name.'

This was what he liked to refer to as an 'emotional coup'.

'We'll have to call it *Sira* then,' replied Brinco, clearly waging an inner war to find the right tone of voice.

'Why not? The name fits!'

The Old Man set off walking, with Carburo behind. Taking care not to step on his shadow. Measuring his distance. Suddenly Mariscal stopped, turned towards the dock and pointed at the boat with his cane. 'Better name it *Sira I.*'

And then, 'Well, aren't you going to try it out?'

The last thing Fins saw was Brinco and Chelín boarding the powerful machine. Brinco taking hold of the steering wheel. And, after turning around, a swarm of bubbles rising and climbing in the night.

23

There was no moon, nor was it expected. A formation of solid storm clouds, brand name the Azores, gave depth to the night's darkness. On the surface of the sea, squeezed between two stones, a vein of graphite clarity. The high-speed customs patrol boat was hidden behind one of the crane boats for gathering mussels, which in turn was moored to a platform under repair. They were waiting for him. For Brinco. The fastest pilot. The estuary ace. A hero to smugglers.

The gurgle of his entrails may have rumbled out across the sea. The customs officer caught him clenching his teeth in an attempt to quell his gut's rebellion. He realised the other man felt unwell, but didn't say anything.

'What, you seasick?'

It was the navigator who asked, with what seemed like inevitable scorn.

'Do I look like the deceased?' said Fins.

'No, just dead for now.'

'When we're on the move, I'll be OK,' he said, feeling like a conspicuous bundle. Then he added with bravura, in an effort to encourage himself, 'The faster the better!'

'Well, now's the time to wait,' remarked the officer. 'Take a deep breath. It's all in the mind.'

Fins didn't have time to explain that he'd been born on a boat, so to speak, during a maritime procession. Something like that. His body's discomfort was a sort of trick or revenge.

The information was first class. Could cure any amount of seasickness.

There he was. Judging by the impressive engine, it could only be him. The kind of boat that was displayed in San Telmo and would suddenly disappear, moments before an inspection. Though recently they'd changed their habits. Started hiding the most valuable speedboats in sheds or warehouses in the most surprising places, sometimes a long way inland, at distances that could be measured in nocturnal miles, on secondary roads. This journey towards secrecy was part of the biggest change ever in the history of smuggling.

From mussel-raft blond to flour.

From tobacco to cocaine.

No, there weren't any billboards advertising this historical change. And there were few superiors ready or willing to hear, let alone believe, his endless storytelling. Fins Malpica was a bloody nuisance, a prick, a lunatic. He should be assigned to investigating UFOs.

The boat turned. Seemed to be moving away with a mocking curtain of foam. But it came back. The ticking-over of the engine, by contrast, was like a whisper in the night. They docked next to platform B-52, exactly the one Fins had indicated. The customs officer and two agents stared with a mixture of admiration and disbelief at this pale young police inspector clinging to his camera as to a child, dressed like an apprentice on his first outing.

'Great, golden information, inspector. My congratulations.'

A surprising informer. A nugget dropped by chance. An angry

person's betrayal of trust. These were the sources the officer turned over in his mind. Fins should have revealed the true story behind platform B-52. The hours upon hours of poring over registers. Analysing operations for buying and selling rafts. Grouping suspicious cases in a 'grey area'. Unravelling the front man and real owner. Use, output, repairs to the structure. A whole series of dead hours and occasional living ones. And there it was, B-52. Real owner, Leda Hortas.

Somebody leaps from the speedboat on to the platform's wooden arbour. Inverno, thinks Fins, because of the way he moves. He opens a trapdoor in one of the platform's large floats. These used to be old drums, hulls or boilers. Now they're made of plastic or metal and look like submersibles. On one of them is Inverno or whoever it is. He climbs into the float with a torch.

'Full speed ahead! Let's go get 'em!' exclaims the customs officer.

This gives rise to shouts of alarm.

The smuggler emerges with a bundle. Skips across the wooden structure. Throws the sack to one of those on board and jumps after it.

A megaphone on the patrol boat orders them to stop. The agents point their weapons. They're in such an advantageous position the pilot will have no problem cutting them off. What they don't expect is such a rash manoeuvre. The speedboat's sudden acceleration, the violent lifting of the nose so that it's almost vertical, almost capsizing, the obvious suicidal wish, impervious to persuasion, to pass straight through the patrol boat.

'The guy's crazy!'

'That bastard's going to kill himself and us!'

The use of their weapons would only make matters worse.

The officer orders an immediate about-turn. The speedboat glances past. Just enough time for Fins to aim his camera. And shoot the flash. A trembling, violent exchange of looks.

It was Brinco, yes, steering the *Sira III*.

24

He used to take her there himself. To Bellissima. The hair salon.
The name had been his idea. He would take her to work every
day. And go and fetch her. He hadn't changed, God damn it, those
loudmouths always holding forth. Swiss accounts. Tax havens.
Then the rumours got published in the press: money has no
homeland. Well, that's right. *Statu quo*. The point is Guadalupe,
his wife, didn't want him to take her any more. She drove herself.
Though the car was one he'd bought. A present. A safe vehicle.
Listen, girl, you spend half your time with your head in the clouds.
A 2002 turbo. A palindrome.

She was sitting down, her feet bare. Her assistant, Mónica, was
giving her a pedicure. You could see the two of them got on well.
It was still early in the morning, a day like any other, and there
weren't any customers. So they were using the time to make themselves look pretty. Quite right. A hairdresser needed to look like a
superstar. Or so he thought. They were married. She'd abandoned
the canning factory and he'd asked her one day, 'Listen, Guadalupe,
what do you want?' She had answered, 'I want to have a trade.'

'Wouldn't a business be better?'

'A business might be better, but I want to have a trade.'

* * *

There were tangos playing on the cassette player. Guadalupe's nails. 'Tinta roja' sung by Goyeneche the Pole. It should be fairly straightforward.

'Go out for a while, would you, girl?' he said to Mónica.

No, it wasn't a lack of trust. But today he preferred to be alone with Guadalupe. He never forgot an anniversary.

'"Red ink in yesterday's grey . . ." How well you used to sing tangos! Remember? The factory foreman shouting, "Sing! All of you, sing!" So you wouldn't put mussels in your mouths. "Sing! Sing!" How pathetic!'

He gave her a jewellery box.

'Well, aren't you going to open it? Go on then . . .'

Guadalupe opened it. Inside was a diamond ring. She closed the box. A little smile. A painful smile. Something was something. A diamond, a tear, etc., etc.

'Our silver wedding anniversary. Twenty-five years. Who'd have thought it?'

He looked at her feet again. Her feet always turned him on. Whenever he mentioned this, there were always idiots who laughed. Well, if they didn't understand, he wasn't going to explain. The two most erotic things in the world? The feet. First the left foot. And then the right.

'You've wonderful feet. I've always been crazy about your feet.'

He was able to touch them. Pass his hand along the instep. Curve the curve. A stroke of bad luck. He didn't know when it happened. When the wind kicked up. She realised he was seeing more than one woman. Or did she?

She got up and put on her sandals. 'Do you need something?'

'A few calls. Just a few calls.'

They weren't so few. Mariscal passed her a ream of

handwritten sheets, with numbers and messages. Those things that sounded so absurd to her. Which she read automatically.

'If you want, we could have dinner somewhere tonight. Some shellfish. Some invertebrates!'

Guadalupe turned to look at him, that itching of the eyes, and took an age to say, 'I don't feel so well. But thanks for thinking of me.'

'Listen, girl. Don't be hard on me. I've only got three or four haircuts left. Maybe less. Do you think I should dye my grey hair? You women are lucky. One day you're blonde, the next you're dark. I like you more with black hair. Because of your skin. You always were a bit swarthy. But we men . . . If I turn up looking blond all of a sudden, I lose my authority. And I was blond, you know. More than blond. I was downright golden, like the setting of the sun. My hair on fire. Like that guy Oliveira introduced to me. Remember? The guy from the PIDE. Mr Arcada. The Legate. Dead Man's Hand. Along came a gust of wind and disturbed his wig. The ugly ones are always the vainest. The worse the wood, the more it grows. So along came this wind and shifted his hairpiece, and there went his authority. Oh, I don't know. He consumes everything, dirty money, weapons, drugs, and still he gives us that sermon about authority, sacred ground. Bloody hell! The twenty-fifth of April, if they'd left it to him, there wouldn't have been a carnation revolution or any other kind. A few cannon blasts in the Terreiro do Paço, a few more in the Carmo, when Captain Salgueiro was there with his megaphone, and things would soon have gone back to normal. I said to him, "*Velis nolis*, Mr Arcada. People have to eat, to have shoes on their feet, not to get beaten, if they're going to be happy, have money in their pockets. If people are fed and in possession of some cash, if they have liquidity, that's good for business. That's my philosophy, Mr

Legate. I like knocking these leeches around. Half the country out working abroad and all day long holding forth about the motherland and empire. That's slandering the communist enemy! Listen, everywhere goes up and down, but I know something about emigration. Half of Galicia is on the outside."

'Then I thought about it. Did a U-turn. This guy was a bastard, but he was *our* bastard. So there and then I came out with a laudation for Salazar and Franco, the two pillars of Western civilisation. Shame about their successors. Marcelo Caetano, a coward. The ones here, traitors. He said the PIDE hadn't been so into torture as other political police forces, such as the Spanish force, to give an obvious example. "I was a Viriathus," he declared. "Nineteen years of age and I left as a volunteer, like thousands of others, to give those reds a beating. I was an out-and-out Crusader. But what I saw, to tell you the truth, made me afraid. A colleague said to me, 'This is dangerous land, Nuno.' And he was right. God was nowhere to be seen. So, being practical, I replied, 'What happened happened.' But he stayed firm. What the PIDE did to detainees was cause them a certain 'absence of comfort'. That was the term. Well, I was taken aback. Torment? No. Absence of comfort." I liked that expression. I took note. Shame I wasn't around to give it to Lame for his dictionary. "Look what I have here, Basilio. What do you make of this one? 'Absence of comfort'." "What does that mean?" "It means torture, Basilio, torture."

'Well, this enlightened bastard, Dead Man's Hand, I have to admit it, was equally refined when it came down to business. Though we got off to a bad start. After the Portuguese revolution, the captains of April, carnations and all that, he escaped to Galicia and took up with another crowd. That was back in 1974, Franco was still alive and the idea was to provoke a squabble between Spain and Portugal. I know because I was one of the people involved. It was a line of business, or so I thought. Weapons were always an option, but things didn't go well and they had to be sold on the cheap. Then, when Cinderello turned his attention to the new life, he ended up showing a talent for business. His experience, old contacts, stuff like that, was pretty useful. And the hairpiece fitted. He looked quite different, to tell the truth. I remember all of that. I'm worried about memory. Everybody complains about their memory. I'm worried I remember too much. I get caught up on names, recollections. And from time to time, that's an absence of comfort.'

Mutatis mutandis, he looked away from Guadalupe Brancana. Felt his presence had lost its triumphal air. In the end said, 'This is the one I need an urgent response for. You can send it via Mónica.' Guadalupe nodded. Mariscal opened the door. Stood still for a moment on the border. One of his favourites was playing, 'Garúa'. That tango about the rain. The two of them were young enough to dance tangos. They didn't care about the murmuring gaze. Then he thought, in relation to himself, that a man could improve himself. He hummed along to the music on the cassette. 'The wind brings a strange lament . . .' Looked one way and then the other, as he always did. Without turning around, let the door close behind him. And since there was no one in sight, either to the left or to the right, he spat on the pavement.

Ex abundantia cordis.

25

Fins stayed close to her for days, stroking her face, without her realising. From a sports boat moored in the harbour he photographed the woman framed in the window. Several moments which struck him as special, in particular those when she appeared in the window with company, he also recorded on film with a Super 8 camera. But the thing he'd never forget – an unknown trembling, his optic nerve setting all the other senses on edge, immersing everything in a strange tense, remembered present – was when yet again he scoured the fronts of the buildings facing the docks and located the window. The woman in the window. Leda Hortas. He tried out the zoom. Focused, unfocused and focused again. A Nikon F with a 70-200 lens like a piercing prolongation. Rude, desirous, infallible. Yes, Leda was the lookout. A photo. The photo. Another. And another.

'You're going to have a change of air, Leda,' the Old Man had said to her one day. 'You're off to the capital.'

'Are you going to give me an apartment then?' she replied slyly. She liked to joke with Mariscal. And he liked to play along. He was an expert in irony.

'You deserve a manor house, girl.'

'That would need a lot of cleaning.'

'With every convenience. A noble palace.'

'Nonsense. All the men around here worship Our Lady of the Fist.'

'It's the memory of the famine, girl. The best enchantments are those that come free. Blessed are the meek, for they shall inherit the earth . . .'

'Right. So what do I have to do in this apartment?'

'Keep your eyes wide open.'

He said this in a very serious tone. Not playing along any more. His voice had changed. He spoke like someone in authority entrusting a mission and expecting to be obeyed.

'Brinco will give you the details.'

From where Leda kept a lookout could be seen the movements of the customs boats arriving and leaving. Next to the window was a small table with a telephone. Which started ringing.

The voice that said hello could only be one voice, and it was. Guadalupe's. Even so, they went through the ritual.

'Is that the home of Domingo?' asked Guadalupe.

'Yes, it is.'

'And how is he?'

'He's OK. But he's resting at the moment. He worked all night.'

'Then I'll call again later.'

'Thank you, madam. That's very kind. I'll expect your call.'

Leda hung up and leaned out of the half-open window. Had another look at the customs patrol boats. Fins remained where he was. Spying on the spy. Zooming in slowly. Taking time over the portrait. Waiting for a look of melancholy. There it was.

'These are good,' said Mara Doval back at the police station, after the photos had been developed. 'You should devote yourself to this full time, become a paparazzo.'

26

Carburo didn't like being rushed. But the boss was impatient today. Rubbing his hands. All he needed now was to start singing 'Mira que eres linda'. Which was what he sang when things were going well. Carburo was familiar with the whole repertoire. The counterpoint came when he hummed 'Tinta roja', for example. Carburo had a fondness for this tango. For the way the Old Man sang it. 'That carmine letter-box, that dive where the Eyetie was crying.' People didn't sing well when they were happy. Exactly the opposite. But today he was in a good mood. 'See how pretty, how lovely you are.' There was nothing he could do about it.

It was his job to start up the radio transceiver and do the talking. Mariscal might sing, but never in public. He never broadcast. He never touched a phone, let alone one of those machines that reached further than he could tell. They were parked in one of his favourite miradors, Cape Vento Soán, which they'd driven to along a secret track surrounded by protective ferns which closed again once they'd passed. At the crossroads, in another vehicle, Lelé kept watch.

Inside the car, Carburo handled the radio transceiver, which had been fitted and camouflaged in the dashboard.

'Ready to go, boss.'

He proceeded to repeat what Mariscal told him word for word, using the International Code of Signals.

'Here Lima Alfa Charlie Sierra India Romeo, calling Sierra India Romeo Alfa Uniform, do you read me? Over.'

'Here Sierra India Romeo Alfa Uniform. We read you loud and clear! Over.'

'Attention. You have to work using the same coordinates as Imos Indo. All clear? Over.'

'OK. Understood. Same coordinates as Imos Indo. So we don't have to wait for Mingos. Over.'

'Correct, correct. That is correct. Mingos is not going. Mingos is resting. He worked all night. Good fishing! Over.'

'OK, understood. We'll be on our way then. Over and out.'

Mariscal bent down next to the window. 'Tell them that this time the wind is fair, there's no room in the sea for all that bass.'

Carburo glanced at the Old Man in surprise. He seemed to be waiting for a translation or confirmation. No one gave messages like that any more. Such nonsense was a thing of the past.

'You're right,' said Mariscal. 'Tell them to come via the shade. Over and out.'

Carburo repeated, 'Come via the shade. Over and out.'

The bodyguard disconnected the transceiver, took down the antenna and closed the false compartment in the dashboard. He got out of the car and stretched like a cat. Rarely had he seen Mariscal so excited. Clearly the bundles were going to be full. There he was, next to the cliff's edge, standing tall, craning his neck, that way he had of helping the binoculars. The speedboats travelled full throttle along two different routes. Rather than sailing on the surface of the sea, they seemed to be jumping from wave to wave. Outside the estuary they would converge in a single direction, towards the mother boat.

'How I wish I could see the *mamma*!' said Mariscal, scanning the horizon.

'Sure, boss. Wouldn't that be nice?'

The day we see the *mamma*, Carburo murmured to himself, we'll be well and truly done for.

27

From the yacht Fins took time to focus on Leda. Almost all the windows were open. Hardly surprising, given how hot it was. He looked around. The way a spy does. Then sought out the presence of Salgueiro, the officer on board the customs patrol boat. There he was, waiting. Fins made the prearranged signal of lifting a green handkerchief to his face. Shortly after that, the patrol boat began to cast off.

When he picked up his camera again, he saw that Leda's window was empty. Just as he'd expected. She didn't take long to return with some binoculars. She focused on where the patrol boats were usually moored. He watched her do so.

Using the powerful zoom, he could see the expression on her face change. To one of surprise, stupor.

Leda made a phone call from her usual position.

On the carpet in the sitting room a child was playing with two dinosaurs, pitting them against each other in a mock battle. He was six years old. This was Santiago, Leda and Víctor's son. He wore a corrective patch over one of his eyes.

'The T-rex will smash you, silly velociraptor.'

Leda told him to lower his voice while quickly dialling a number. At the other end, in the hair salon, Guadalupe picked up.

'Is Mr Lima there? It's urgent.'

'No, Mr Lima is out, but I can give him a message.'

'This is Domingo's wife. Tell him Domingo, Mingos, left for work. Left in a hurry. Is already refreshed. This is urgent.'

'Understood.'

Guadalupe scribbled a note, balancing the receiver on her shoulder.

She covered the receiver and gestured to Mónica, 'Quick! Take this to Mariscal. And give it to him personally.'

Leda made sure the customs boat had left the port. She lit a cigarette, sat down on the wretched imitation leather sofa, that nightmare of hers, getting stuck and not being able to get up. She tried to distract herself by watching her son play.

Fins decided to wait. Now he was the man in the empty window. Time became eternal when Leda was out of sight. This was an absence he couldn't manage. For which there was no medicine. Except for something new in the surroundings. Like this. A red Rover. Brinco had one that was the same model. The car parked at an angle to the kerb, next to the docks. Yes, Leda had a visitor. Brinco always walked a couple of feet in front when Chelín was with him. They had two ways of walking that were very different. Brinco in a straight line, striding fast, sometimes jangling the car or house keys. Chelín trying to keep up, glancing from side to side, noticing the occasional detail. A shop window. Some graffiti. Which is why, in almost all the photos Fins took that day, Chelín is more visible. As if he was posing or something.

Leda heard a noise in the lock and started. There was a small hallway which led directly into the sitting room where she was and where she had her lookout position next to the window. Brinco always entered like this. He never rang. Never warned he was coming. He went up to her and gave her a hug.

The first thing Chelín noticed was the patch Santiago was

wearing over one eye. 'Don't tell me you turned out cross-eyed, Santi?'

Brinco heard the unusual question and turned towards his son. 'What happened to him?'

'Nothing happened to him. It's to make him better. Doctor's orders.'

Chelín burst out laughing. 'Blimey, squinty!'

'It's called strabismus,' said Leda. 'He's strabismic.'

Brinco bent down and observed the child's free eye slowly. He then stood up and pointed at Chelín very seriously. 'It's not a squint! You heard his mother. It's . . .'

'Extremism,' said Chelín ironically, managing to suppress his laughter.

'Strabismus, you fool, strabismus!'

'It's nothing serious,' continued Leda. 'Fortunately the people at school realised. He has a lazy eye. One sees better than the other. You have to cover the good one so that the other does some work.'

'That's the way of the world, lad!' declared Víctor solemnly. 'The truth is the patch looks good on you.'

'It looks great!'

'Why don't you take him for a walk?' said Brinco to Chelín.

'Sure thing. Come on, you. Let's go give that lazy eye something to do.'

The inspector watched Chelín leave with Leda's son. They were messing around. Fins thought he knew the boy well. He realised Chelín sometimes took on the role of general and court jester. They got in the car. He wondered whether to follow them or stay behind. Deep down, though, he already knew what he was going to do.

He looked up at the window and aimed his zoom.

Víctor and Leda were kissing.

Fins couldn't stop photographing them. His eye and pulse had gone beyond any mission. The couple unconsciously obeyed the camera's every wish. The way Leda turned towards the window. Brinco embraced her from behind. The way they made love on top of the harbour, bounding over the city's hills.

He waited before returning to Noitía. He wanted to be alone in the police station, no questions or inquisitive looks when he came out of the darkroom. He certainly wasn't expecting Mara Doval to still be there. That may have been one of the reasons he held back. But there she was, reading, like one of those students who wait for the lights to go out before leaving the library.

'How was the session?'

'OK. He turned up. He finally turned up.'

'I want to see that couple!'

Before he went into the darkroom, Mara said she had some important news. The phone in Leda's apartment only received and made calls to a single number. And that number belonged to a public establishment.

'Which one?'

'Bellissima, Bellissima!' she laughed enigmatically.

Fins closed the door behind him. Turned on the red light.

He didn't know quite where he was, where he'd come from, what he was doing with these carnal prints in his hands, which emitted the groans of a pair of lovers. But Mara Doval hadn't moved. She looked annoyed. Professional.

'Next time, inspector, close the door more slowly.'

'It was a long time ago.'

'I don't want to see any more of your paparazzo photos. What I want you to see now are mine. You didn't let me finish. Apart from Bellissima, Bellissima, I have some other news. If the inspector is interested.'

'There were two twin cars. Two Alfa Romeos. Nuova Giuliettas. I noticed because I like them. That badge with the serpent and dragon's head. Yes, you told me the other day, I like the same cars as mafia bosses. I also like Portuguese tiles. Which is why we were there, Berta and I. Berta the painter. Yes, she also likes cats, but I have one whereas she must have a dozen. Her studio's full of cats, mostly stray ones. No, she doesn't paint them. She takes inspiration from their eyes, or so she says. It's wonderful watching how attentive they are while she paints. She only ever uses primary colours. Reds. Both Nuova Giuliettas were red. Hang on, wait a minute. Be patient. So we went to Caminha railway station to see the nineteenth-century murals. You should go and see them, really you should. That's the only reason my shutter was open. I know they say that if you're on a case, you should never close your shutter. But yesterday was my day off, and I didn't want it open. My primary objective was to go and eat cod in Viana do Castelo. No, not à la Margarida da Praça, nor à la Gomes de Sá. In the end what I had, let's see if I can remember, was "sliced cod with maize bread on a bed of baked potatoes and salted turnip tops". Mnemosyne never forgets. And then we stopped in Afife, at Cabanas Convent, Homem de Mello's place. Yes, the one who wrote "Povo que lavas no rio". Isn't that the best *fado* ever? "Chaves da vida"? No, I haven't heard that one. How strange! Our next stop was Caminha station, the one with the tiles.

'Which is where our story begins. So just be patient.

'Berta was driving. I don't know anything about that. I'm the co-pilot, the one with the maps, leaflets and so on. We were just about to enter the station, through the door, when I looked to my right. A red Nuova Giulietta with a Spanish number plate. Pretty, too. We went to see the tiles in the station. They're amazing, as I told you. We took some photographs. Went to see a train that was arriving. No problems. We must have been there about an hour. We were just about to leave, coming through the door of the station, when suddenly the Shutter of my Imagination opened. I grabbed Berta. Said to her, "Wait, wait, the car park." The Nuova Giulietta was on my right. With a group of four people standing beside it. But Mnemosyne knows that the Nuova Giulietta was on the other side, on her right when she came in. So it was. I peeked through the glass door and saw the other Giulietta. They had exactly the same number plate, both of them with a Spanish registration. So I said, "Berta, I'm going to take a portrait of you à la Andy Warhol. Fool around a little." I love Polaroids. They make a lot of noise, but nothing you can't disguise by pretending to be tourists. No heavy machinery, mind you. Not like others.'

'Right. So what happened?'

'Two youngish-looking men got into one Giulietta and an older couple got into the other. And went their separate ways. One pair towards the border. The other in the direction of Viana de Castelo. What do you think then?'

'A real fairy tale. Let me see those photos!'

Fins immediately recognised the two younger men. A magnificent couple who were clearly on the same wavelength. The estuary ace and his lawyer. Víctor Rumbo and, in glasses, Óscar Mendoza.

'Who are the others? That strange-looking man . . . and the woman in mourning. That waxen face. They look as if they've just come out of Tenebrae, having sung the Miserere.'

'What makes him look so strange? He's just a well-dressed old man in a tie.'

'I don't know. That waxen face . . . There's something strange about it.'

'He's wearing a wig,' said Mara. 'That's what it is. It's not so unusual to wear a wig.'

'On him it looks like some kind of geographical feature.'

'He's called Dead Man's Hand,' she said suddenly. 'Do you want to know more?'

'Yes.' Fins nodded. She was right, as always. You had to be patient.

Nuno Arcada, Dead Man's Hand, had worked for the PIDE, the dictator Salazar's secret police. He wasn't a run-of-the-mill policeman. He'd been assigned abroad for several years, most of the time in France. He'd infiltrated several groups in exile and also belonged to various emigrants' associations with trade-union or cultural concerns. This was how he obtained information, not only about them, but also about what was going on back in Portugal.

'He hunted inside and out,' said Mara Doval. 'And inside he had his own, very special hand, which he used during interrogations. He's said to have been an expert in electricity. Obviously he had some very good Spanish friends with similar interests and occupations. This collaboration enabled him to go into hiding in Galicia after the Carnation Revolution. And it opened up several lines of business for him afterwards.'

'The cars! It was an exchange. Probably the one Dead Man's Hand was driving is the one with the upholstery. Financial, of course.'

'That money's in heaven by now!'

'I'm impressed, Miss Mnemosyne. Did you mention this to the Portuguese Judiciary Police?'

'No.'

'No? You know there are some good people . . .'

'Yes. But it was one of Berta's cats who recognised the old man in the photo and told me his story. A Portuguese journalist. Working for the *Jornal de Notícias*. He's been studying the PIDE's crimes for years. Anything else?'

'Yes, talk to me about Bellissima, please!'

28

Chelín took Santiago to a deserted beach in Bebo, the typical sort of cove that knows how to stay hidden, but when it's found, opens like a shell. The path meandered between old stone walls protecting impossible crops. They'd obviously been erected by some intelligent mind because they had strategic holes for the wind to escape through. Which made them a bit nosy. Cabbages peered through. Sometimes sent the odd, restless bird to have a look. A black redstart, for example.

A haven of peace. A good firing range.

At the end of the path, where it met the beach, was an abandoned rusty road sign. A triangle with a red border. Inside the triangle, a black cow on a white background.

'The things the sea comes up with!'

Chelín lifted the sign and placed some stones around its base to keep it upright.

'I'm going to teach you the second most important thing a man should know.'

He took out the pistol he wore hidden on his back, next to his waist, under his jacket.

'Something else the sea came up with,' remarked Chelín with an ironic smile.

His ease calmed the boy's initial amazement. He stopped next to him. Both of them eyed the sign. The cow. The man bent down and placed his right knee on the sand. Then wrapped his arms around the boy, helping him to hold the weapon and take aim.

'That's right, with gentleness,' said Chelín, who set about preparing the weapon as he was speaking. 'Do you know its name? Astra Llama. Nice, isn't it? It's a special one, with wooden grips. Everybody wants mother-of-pearl grips, but wood's better. Wood is more loyal.'

'Did the sea really give it to you?'

He gave free rein to his voice, he wasn't quite sure why. It must have been as a result of removing the safety catch.

'Actually I got it from a dealer. You know what a dealer is, don't you? Someone who deals cards. Well, there's another sort of dealer, one who deals in smack.'

Santiago laughed, repeated the word 'smack'.

The man clicked his tongue. He had a big mouth that sometimes sounded off for him.

'That's right. We'll go and see him one day. But in the meantime, don't tell anyone about him. All right?'

He stared at the sea. The jumping of the waves. The waves' mane. The beating surf, piercing sound. Exhaled. Focused. Set the trigger.

'Nature's amazing, Santi. The blessed host in verse. Now let's take aim. Let's blast that cow out of the skies.'

The shot reached its target. Left a perfect hole in the cow's flank. To start with, the triangular sign groaned, as if wanting to avoid the fall.

'Again, Santi!'

The wind fingered the new hole. Took it calmly. The sign finally succumbed to its fate.

'See? Your lazy eye's working already.'

Standing up, Chelín kissed his weapon and put it away.

Looked around. Ruffled the child's hair. Smiled. Turned towards the sea and unzipped his trousers.

'Come on, champ! With style. Legs apart. Looking ahead, but keeping an eye on the dicky bird. Never into the wind. The birdie has to ride out the storm.'

Chelín laughed as he watched the rigorous, disciplined way in which the boy copied his movements. He then stood upright, looking martial, eyes to the front, to give the solemn message:

'And this is the first thing a man should know. How not to get piss on his trousers!'

'I'm fed up of counting boats,' said Leda.

They were still together, next to the window. In the urban dusk it was the eyes that switched on the lights in a succession of candles. Unlike other cities, Atlántica grew at night. Next to the docks and in the estuary, the small lights on the cranes, showing the position of vessels, green and red, implied the hybrid awakening of animal and machine, the movements of a remarkable somnambulist.

Leda moved away from Brinco. Took out a cigarette and lit it. 'Fed up of everything!'

The woman returning to the frame of the window underlined her exclamation by blowing out smoke. She added with a hint of scorn, 'Fed up of this sofa, most of all! You end up feeling like your whole body is imitation leather.'

'Soon you'll live in a palace,' affirmed Brinco. They'd had this conversation before, but this time he had an air of determination.

'Oh yes? What palace?'

'Your own! I'll take care of that. Don't you worry! With a large pool. So you can swim on your own like a mermaid.'

'Better give it an outlet to the sea. Mermaids prefer the sea.'

'I'm being serious. You won't have to keep a lookout any more.'

'So how you going to do that?'

'If I were Mariscal, I'd have paid off the customs chief by now.'

'Then what are you waiting for?'

29

It's a beautiful spring day on the coast. Sunny, but windy as well. The east wind not only ruffles the sea, but for the first time after the long winter seems to want to distance it from the earth with gusts that whirl about its surface. It gathers up all the greens, pulling them in different directions. But this wind encourages the light, a succession of flashes, which perhaps lessens resistance and promotes sympathy.

We can see all of this with the help of Sira.

We can see it through the window in the Ultramar's master bedroom. The largest, the one with the best views. The one known as La Suite. She is sitting on one side of the bed. Dressed. As she watches, she loosens her hair, which was tied up in a bun. The thing with windows that have the best view is they pique the curiosity of what they're looking at. Here they come. To see Sira.

As her hair unfolds and falls, she appears hieratic, expressionless, but everything on the outside, starting with the wind and the restless light, is in the eyes. Sira watches a car on the coastal road moving slowly, as if wanting to linger over the potholes. It's Mariscal's white Mercedes. It passes in front of a clothes line where the yellow shirts and black shorts and socks of the Noitía football team are hanging out to dry like flashing pennants.

On the ground floor, in the bar of the Ultramar, closed at this hour of the afternoon, Rumbo is using a white cloth to wipe a glass. From time to time the wind can be heard whistling and an old iron sign creaking. The barman's wearing spectacles. The way he's polishing the glass even the most casual observer would describe as obsessive. He lifts it to the light, stares at it, as if seeking a sporadic stain that hides and then reappears.

Rumbo's intensive work is interrupted by Mariscal knocking at the door. Rumbo can see his face on the other side, behind the thin curtain with lace edges. He's dressed like an emigrant in a white linen suit, a red bow tie and a thin straw hat. His cane is hanging off his arm by the handle.

Rumbo takes one last look at the glass and places it upside down on the counter, on top of a white cloth, next to the other polished glasses.

He makes his way to the door. He's wearing a white apron. Before he opens up, the two men exchange looks through the gap in the curtain. The barman seems to hesitate, looks down at the lock, but carries on anyway, takes the key from his pocket and quickly opens the door.

Mariscal's cough could be understood as a greeting. Quique Rumbo turns around and goes to switch on the television. He presses the button with the end of a broom handle. A meteorological map appears on the screen, complete with isobars.

Mariscal glances at Rumbo, Rumbo's back, the television in the background, and starts to climb the stairs.

'They haven't a fucking clue,' he says. 'Here they never get it right. We're *terra incognita* for them! Tomorrow's the first of April, there'll be drum rolls in the sky . . .'

Rumbo keeps his position. Doesn't comment. Meanwhile Mariscal continues with his forecast in a monotone, as if trying

to disguise the percussion of his feet on the wooden steps.
'. . . and the first spiders will start to weave their webs.'

He moves slowly through the chiaroscuro of the landing. There are lamps on the walls now with green shades, and a series of small pictures showing English country scenes, horsemen chasing after foxes. A job lot. All of which gives the impression of a colonial setting, provisional screens, that fluttering of the curtains as they're lifted by the wind. A tunnel of flags, he thinks. Don't they ever shut the blasted windows? He stops at the door to the suite, at the far end of the landing. Hangs his cane from the wrist of his left hand and slowly removes the white gloves. It's the first time we see his bare hands with the old burn scars on the back. His right hand hovers in the air for a moment. Eventually he knocks gently. Takes a handkerchief from his pocket to hold the handle and open the door.

Sira doesn't move when Mariscal comes in. She still has her gaze on the seascape outside the window. Mariscal looks at her and then follows her gaze. Without saying a word, he goes to the other side of the bed. Sits down, wipes his brow with his handkerchief, that tic he has, and carelessly stuffs it into his breast pocket.

'There'll be a storm tomorrow.'

On the wall, on wallpaper decorated with acanthus leaves, is a souvenir picture showing a wooden bridge in Lucerne covered in flowers, with the Alps in the background. Mariscal stares at it, as if he's only just discovered it's there, this photograph of flowers and snow.

'We should go somewhere together. At some point.'

Sira doesn't reply. She carries on gazing at the seascape outside the window. The wind is there, beating with a world of things on its back. Mariscal stands up. Goes to wash his hands in a bowl on top of the chest of drawers. Before doing so, he takes a couple of sachets from his pocket and pours the contents into the water. As the grains mix with the water they produce a kind of bubbling, and that is when Mariscal places his hands inside the bowl. In the meantime:

'There are places that are a wonder, Sira. You always wanted to go to Lisbon, I know. All your life singing *fados*, and we never went to Lisbon. "In the Madragoa district, in Lisbon's window, Rosa Maria was born . . ." We have to go to the Alfama during the feast of St Anthony, Sira! We never even went to Madrid! I could take you to a good hotel. The Palace, the Ritz. To the Opera. The Prado Museum. Yes, the museum . . .'

In the bar on the ground floor, Quique Rumbo stares at himself in one of the vertical mirrors that flank the central shelf of bottles. In the mirror frame is a cover plate concealing a lock. Rumbo takes a key from his pocket and slowly unlocks the mirror door. Inside is a weapon. A double-barrelled shotgun. And a pack of cartridges. Rumbo takes two cartridges and loads the weapon.

Mariscal bends down, looks at the ground. He's searching in his memory, and his voice becomes more grave.

'The truth is, it had never occurred to me to enter the Prado, but the meeting was there. Something to do with Italians, I thought. But what a piece of luck, Sira, what a marvel. Museums are the best places in the world. Better than natural landscapes. Better than the Grand Canyon or Everest, I'm telling you. Always at the same temperature. The climate is ideal.'

Something is happening on the other side of the bed. Sira's gaze is now that of someone trying to stem her tears.

'It's because of the paintings. The temperature has to be . . . constant. Paintings are very delicate, you know. More than people. We cope with hot and cold much better than paintings. Funny, isn't it? A scene with snow cannot withstand the cold as well as we can. We're the strangest thing in the universe, Sira. Remember those people who used to go fishing for cod in Newfoundland? They'd stick breadcrumbs between their fingers so their skin wouldn't fall off. And on their genitals. They say nothing burns like the cold. That must be true! That girl whose mouth was dry and she stuck her tongue on a block of ice, remember? She couldn't get it off, had to call for help . . . Who'd have believed it?'

He opens the drawer of the bedside table and rummages around. There's plenty to rummage through. His postcards, perhaps?

Basilio Barbeito spent his final days here. So he'd be more comfortable. His presence has had a lasting effect on the room. This is something Mariscal and Sira share without mentioning it. From his time in the room, he left a shelf of handwritten notebooks as an inheritance. All from the same factory, Miquelrius. All the entries for his poor, infinite dictionary are there, in alphabetical order. Write, he wrote everywhere.

Mariscal sits down again on the bed. Leans over towards the woman. Strokes, gently tugs her hair. Lame was in the habit of putting everything to good use. His pockets were always full of words. He wrote on envelopes, on the back of cinema programmes, on bus tickets, scraps of brown paper from the shop, on the palms of his hands, like a child. He didn't leave his hands behind, of course, just the sensation of written skin. Everything full of scraps of paper. The drawer overflowing with word worms.

'Call me names, Sira. That encourages an old man like me. Pimp, mangy dog, rogue, crook, swindler, lech, toothless, serpent, bastard, Beelzebub, whoreson, entrepreneur, son of the four letters, beast . . . archaic! Out of date. No, out of date, no. Archaic's a good one. And beast is even better.'

Mariscal falls silent. Curls Sira's hair in his fingers. An electrifying pleasure for him. Like the first day Guadalupe cut his hair, the way she swept over his temples. Shame about the hairdresser. Some people are like that, they never settle down, are never content. They still sleep together. He occasionally mounts her. But she's not on fire. She doesn't burn. Like a fridge. That's what I say. Memory is a discomfort, that's right, time decays, all those words in the drawer, when suddenly the door opens.

Quique Rumbo. With agitated breathing. The wind has finally found a way in. Sira and Mariscal turn their heads towards him, but otherwise remain still where they are. To begin with, Rumbo takes aim at Sira, but then he hesitates, swings the weapon around until he has Mariscal in his sights.

Finally he turns the gun against himself. Presses it against his chin. And fires.

Reverberates.

Everything's gone. The wind towards the landing.

Trickles of blood run down the veins of the acanthus leaves on the wallpaper. Drops fall from the ceiling. Mariscal stretches out his hand. Where the hell are these drops coming from? From the ceiling, right. He hadn't thought about that. The way dripping blood is silent.

'Don't cry, Sira. I'll take care of everything. He died because he wanted to!'

Per se.

30

'Two Celtic kings, let's say, are playing chess on top of a hill while their troops are out fighting. The battle ends, but the kings carry on playing. This is an image I like a lot. You're a king, Brancana. On top of the hill. Let the pawns do the fighting!'

They were in Delmiro Oliveira's office, an artificial tower with its own terrace, from which the guests could enjoy a broad panorama of the Miño estuary with its islets. It was a good distance from the voices of the partygoers occupying the garden and rooms of the house in Quinta da Velha Saudade, only partly visible from the river, protected by high walls and screens of vegetation, mostly bougainvilleas in flower.

It was the host's seventy-fifth birthday, though this was an excuse. He was happy at home and it seemed ridiculous to celebrate the falling of leaves. But he'd received a call, he didn't let on about this, and made the most of the occasion. Around his desk, apart from Mariscal and Macro Gamboa, the silent Galician partner with him, were the lawyer Óscar Mendoza, the Italian Tonino Montiglio, and Fabio, known to his friends as the Elephant, a Colombian who lived in Madrid, but who'd recently spent a period in Galicia. His nickname was a result of the enthusiasm he'd shown for a cheerful establishment in Lisbon, O Elefante Branco.

They would soon head down to the banquet, where there would be toasts for the future. But now they were concerned with the present. Mariscal understood that the present had largely to do with him. He'd been welcomed with encouraging hugs, following the death of Rumbo in the Ultramar. 'A misfortune. A breakdown, Mariscal. People break down.' He'd remained silent. This mechanical diagnosis didn't give him much comfort. One breakdown leads to another, etc., etc. He was too old to think about committing suicide. Besides, he didn't have the guts to shit so high. Or so he thought to begin with. What to do? *Ite, Missa est.*

'You'll always have Mendoza to apply a bandage rather than a wound,' his host continued. 'To avoid further misfortunes. There's nothing worse for a firm than hatred between factions. The firm looks after everybody. Factions plunder on their own.'

'That's true,' said Mendoza. 'The merit of my profession consists not in winning lawsuits, as people think, but in avoiding them. It's a question of seeking out allies, not enemies.'

'And how's the new captain of the fleet?' asked Fabio.

'He has courage . . . and ambition.'

Delmiro Oliveira seemed to come to at this point, with that capacity he had for walking between the audible and the inaudible, and made his own connection between the two nouns, 'Courage and ambition? Misfortunes never come singly.'

All his jokes, uttered in a serious tone, like those of good comedians, had their meaning. Were acts in themselves. So Mariscal laughed along with the others until the laughter died down.

'That's right. He has courage. Too much perhaps. The wolf will have to learn how to be a fox, isn't that so, Mendoza? On Galician coats of arms there are plenty of wolves and not enough foxes. Then it turned out there were too many foxes and not enough wolves. Or vice versa.'

'I think he's inherited the best of both animals,' declared Mendoza. 'He possesses an innate talent that will go hand in hand with his ambition.'

'Before coming here, I managed to talk to Palindrome,' said Fabio mysteriously. 'Do you know what he said, Mariscal? He said, "Mariscal is like Napoleon."'

'Napoleon?'

'That's what he said. But he added something that impressed me. First of all, "Power needs shade." And then, "There's no shade better than power." I think the same, Mariscal.'

'That's what we all think, isn't it?'

Mendoza's immediate response. The others' agreement, despite Macro Gamboa's silence, meant, Mariscal could tell, that there'd been some kind of consultation in which he hadn't taken part.

'The time has passed for being thieves in the night,' continued Oliveira. 'What's that saying, Tonino?'

'*Il potere logora chi non ce l'ha.*'

Mariscal blew out his cigar smoke with the enthusiasm of someone wishing to make a point.

'That's right, power wears out those who don't have it. What are you thinking, counsellor?'

'That now's the time.'

Mendoza had an instinct for historic opportunities. When he heard the name of Napoleon, his most diligent neurones headed for what he called the Hippocampus Department of Locksmithery. A lock opened, and he couldn't help thinking about one of his favourite books, the one Karl Marx wrote about the Eighteenth Brumaire, not of the first Napoleon, but of Louis Napoleon. The locksmith was working. One door opened another.

He had paragraphs in his memory. The day he brought them out at a meeting of the law faculty, he learned how to spot the gloss of his discourse, the effect of his words on the resonance of bodies, the facial tics of those in disagreement. He remembered they got not only a caricature of the old Napoleon, but the old Napoleon in caricature.

'Now's the time. Everybody's talking about the crisis. Politicians are afraid, discredited. In polls they're dismissed as part of the problem. In the eyes of most people they're incompetent and corrupt, they've got shit stuck in their hair and are unable to rid themselves of this manure, this reputation . . . The noise of swords is constantly heard in the barracks.'

As he spoke, Mendoza noticed that first, pleasurable moment of intoxication produced by saliva with the cereal of language. A fermenting that is only possible when it is shared. As a student, during the dictatorship, he'd defended revolutionary ideas. He'd avoided 'jumps', public demonstrations, and more or less risky acts such as spreading leaflets, putting up posters and spraying walls with graffiti. That was to play a game of cat-and-mouse with a superior brute force. The dictatorship was in ruins, had the same illness as the dictator, multiple sclerosis with a rotting of the internal organs. The real task consisted in forming senior management for the future, for the day after the taking of power. He'd prepared, avoided having fights with the police. Attended class in a suit and tie, availed himself of the services of shoe-shiners. His appearance surprised people at meetings, especially when he opened his mouth and produced an eloquent, radical discourse whose main target was no longer the tottering regime, so old its teeth were falling out, but the revisionists, the social democrats, the puppets of capitalism.

Everything can be put to good use. It had been useful

training. For the first time he felt on his fingertips the clear sensation of being able to control vital threads.

'It's time the king ascended the hill and moved the pieces without being in the thick of battle. It's time, yes,' said the lawyer, preparing with the dynamo of his hands a remark that would bring the conciliabule to a close and hoist him on to Mariscal's shoulders. 'As the ancients used to say, *Hic Rhodus, hic salta!* That's right, gentlemen. Here is Rhodes, jump here!'

Mariscal appreciated the tribute and nodded thoughtfully. His head had to cope with the weight of the crown. And it leaned on its temples for support.

'There's a level here,' he said finally. 'This is what makes it nice to work with people!'

Macro Gamboa had remained silent, with his hands between his legs. He'd worked for a long time transporting things by land and sea and had risen to the condition of businessman on his own merits. He hadn't once glanced at the landscape. He seemed more interested in the others' shoes. Their oscillating movements.

It was some time before his hoarse voice emerged from his inhospitable mouth.

'What the hell are we talking about?'

31

On the right of his desk, Óscar Mendoza had a large globe. The lawyer was standing up, watching it and making it turn. Víctor Rumbo was sitting opposite.

'You've gone quiet, what's the matter?'

'I have an opinion, but it hasn't got to my head yet.'

The lawyer smiled. He recognised the quip. This was one of his standard jokes about Galicians. Mendoza thought he'd have to change this habit of his. Telling jokes about Galicians. Yes, they laughed at their jokes, but then they chewed the words in a corner, as cows chew the cud. No, he wasn't going to say that aloud. Besides, Víctor had a quick temper. Not for nothing was he called Brinco. He would jump out of his seat, react to the slightest provocation. If they cut off his arms, he'd row with his teeth. Better this way. No turning sharp corners, no dropping hints, no change of heart. He hated all that wrong-footing in the dance. Brinco was determined. His ambition was clear to see. Obviously much more of a wolf than a fox. They understood each other. And would get closer all the time.

'That Brinco's crazy,' he'd said once to Mariscal about Víctor Rumbo. It was true he'd done something crazy, unloading a boat in broad daylight. But what the lawyer wanted to know was what the Old Man really thought. They called him that and he didn't mind.

So when Mariscal remained silent, he rephrased his statement: 'To do what he did, you have to be off your rocker. It won't be easy to defend him if he carries on like this.'

'Did he burn some money?' said Mariscal abruptly.

'Why would he burn some money?' asked Mendoza in surprise.

'Well, if he didn't burn any money, then he's not crazy.'

That was the end of Brinco's mental check-up. The one sitting opposite Mendoza. The madman who didn't burn any money and was going to be his henchman. His right-hand man.

'Anyway, no more being the Atlantic's fastest pilot. You're a captain now. You have to take better care of your spine.'

The lawyer pushed the globe with his forefinger, making it spin, but this time more slowly. 'We've a long journey ahead of us. But first you should go and see the Old Man, Víctor.'

'I see him every day!' he replied sombrely. 'He's my favourite ghost.'

'You're like a son to him . . .'

It was Brinco who approached the globe now and gave it a shove. 'What do you mean, like a son? If I'm going to be your boss, don't go talking to me like some idiot out of a soap opera!'

'If the client doesn't agree with the discourse, one has to change the discourse.'

Mendoza pushed the globe in the other direction, his voice seeming to slide all over it. 'Confucius travelled somewhere and was told, "Straightness rules in this kingdom. If a father steals something, the son turns him in; if the son steals something, the father turns him in." Confucius replied, "Straightness also rules in my kingdom. There the son covers up for his father and the father covers up for his son."'

At this point in time, Mendoza would have liked to have Mariscal before him. He would have come out with some Latin, appreciated the elevation in style.

'Got you, Confucius,' barked Brinco before slamming the door behind him. As he did with cars. Something that made Mendoza very nervous.

32

Fins Malpica was driving an unmarked car along the coastal road. He was accompanied by Lieutenant Colonel Humberto Alisal of the Civil Guard, who'd come from Madrid in plain clothes. They were heading for the barracks in Noitía. It was an inspection without prior warning.

'Where are you from, inspector?'

'I was born here, sir. Nearby. In a fishing village in Noitía. A de Meus.'

'Do your parents still live here?'

'My father died some time ago. At sea . . .'

'Oh, I'm sorry.'

'A stick of dynamite went off in his hands.'

When he gave this detail, something he endeavoured to do as quickly as possible, Fins knew there would be an infinite moment, something like the pause between the ticking of a clock.

'Oh!'

It was raining lightly. Fins allowed the windscreen wiper to introduce a couple of asides. Then he expanded on the information. 'My mother's still alive. She has problems managing her memory. Of memory loss, I should say.'

'Alzheimer's is terrible,' remarked Lieutenant Colonel Alisal.

'My mother had it. She'd mix me up with the weatherman! Blow kisses whenever he appeared on television . . .' He made the contained gesture of someone blowing a kiss from the palm of his hand. 'I don't know how she made that association.'

'Maybe the weatherman's pointer and the staff of office,' said Fins.

Humberto Alisal laughed and shook his head. 'No, she never saw me with a staff of office.'

Fins was about to say something about body language, but they were reaching their destination. He slowed down. The windscreen wiper groaned out of laziness. From the car park where they came to a halt they could hear the low panting of the sea muffled by blasts of errant water.

The car park opposite the Civil Guard barracks was full of mostly new, top-of-the-range cars. Given that this was a restricted space, it made the conglomeration of luxury vehicles even more obvious. The contrast between the one Fins Malpica had just parked, his Citroën Dyane, and the others was like that between a barge and a fleet of high-class yachts.

Once out of the vehicle, with Fins behind him, Lieutenant Colonel Alisal seemed to be giving the impressive sedans the once-over. His was a silent review that didn't conceal his displeasure. He walked slowly, paying careful attention to the minor details, starting with the number plates, all of which indicated that the cars had only just been bought. 'This is shameful!'

Fins had been hugely surprised when Superintendent Carro called him into his office to inform him of Alisal's visit and request that he should accompany him. Ever since, on a different trail, he'd located these 'trout in the milk', he'd been in touch with Chief Superintendent Freire of the Civil Guard. The kind of guy he trusted, with whom he would have entered the heart of darkness. Freire paid an undercover visit. And was the one who informed his superiors.

'It hurt me to discover the truth, sir. To start with, I tried to look the other way, but more and more trout kept appearing in the milk. So then I spoke to Chief Superintendent Freire. He came here incognito. Saw first hand what there was.'

'Trout, you say? You're far too polite. Are they all this filthy?'

'No, sir. There are three clean ones. They had a bad time.'

'A bad time? Why? Because they were carrying out their duty?'

'They're off sick. Severe depression.'

'Depression!'

Lieutenant Colonel Alisal marched towards the barracks building. His indignation could be heard moving through the gears. As he walked, he expressed his thoughts aloud, 'Three honourable, sick men. Well, that is something!' Suddenly he stopped and turned to Fins. 'What's going on here? Please explain it to me.'

Fins was always at the ready, but even so he couldn't pinpoint the right answer. He might have said, 'Corruption, sir, and this is just the tip of the iceberg.' But he didn't like to be direct. He was never that direct. Lieutenant Colonel Alisal gazed up at the front of the building, the motto 'All for the Fatherland', and then sought out the sea's horizon. It was a thick, dark, oily sea, across which slid and swept a ragged bunch of clouds.

'All of this on account of some tobacco and a handful of drugs?'

'That's prehistory, sir.'

'But the statistics . . . This doesn't comply with the statistics. We've increased the number of seizures.'

The lieutenant colonel stopped in front of the guard standing sentry at the entrance to the building.

'I wish to talk to the superintendent on duty. At once!'

The guard raised his eyebrows. He didn't like that tone, especially coming from a civilian.

'At once? Who are you then, the Generalissimo?'

The lieutenant colonel took his papers out of the inner pocket of his jacket.

'I am Lieutenant Colonel Party Pooper.'

The guard checked his papers. Immediately stood to attention.

'At your orders, sir!'

He was about to call the sergeant in the guardroom. Tell him to find the superintendent as quickly as possible. But this plain-clothes superior didn't seem too worried about formalities. He had other obsessions. 'Tell me, which of these cars is yours?'

The guard glanced at the third man, who had remained silent. He knew him from somewhere, but couldn't quite place him. He had the appearance of a shadow. Fins, however, knew who the guard was. One clue had led to another without him even trying. Most of the cars had been bought from the same dealer. They hadn't even bothered to cover their tracks. The owner shared business interests with Mariscal. Though the latter wasn't exactly crazy about cars. He still drove his 1966 Mercedes-Benz. Its tail fins formed part of the Wild West landscape.

'Are you happy, does it run well?'

'I can't complain. The car runs well. If you increase your speed, the consumption goes up. But I'm not one to do that.'

'At ease!'

'Thank you very much, sir.'

33

'An interview? What for, counsellor? *Cui prodest?*'

'You do. You stand to gain. You're a gentleman, you can't go down in history as a cattle thief.'

Óscar Mendoza had already accepted on his behalf. An image campaign, he explained. *Cui prodest. Cui bono*, etc., etc. He had nothing to lose. On the contrary, everything to gain.

'I already have a good image,' countered Mariscal. 'I'm known as a bit of a Casanova.'

The lawyer played along. 'That's right, but it could be bettered. Do you know what Churchill used to say? "History will be kind to me, for I intend to write it."'

'Who said that?'

'Churchill,' repeated Mendoza. 'Winston Churchill.'

'I know who Churchill is, counsellor!'

Mariscal used this occasion to tell a story with mocking familiarity. 'My father sold him wolfram at a good price. He sold it to the others as well. The Nazis wanted wolfram to make weapons and the Brits to stop them. On occasion, like other people, my father would sell the same material twice.'

'A real neutral!' exclaimed Mendoza.

That's right. A neutral. Many border fortunes had been amassed as a result of this mineral needed for Hitler's cannons.

Mutatis mutandis. He rather liked the idea of an image campaign. He touched his neck with his hand, pinched the skin of his double chin. The last time he'd come face to face with a journalist had been to give him a warning. Right there, on the chin.

'They say you're the perfect example of a self-made man, Mr Brancana.'

'Don't beat about the bush. Call me Mariscal.'

He stared at the journalist in silence. Made out he was considering her statement when in fact he was thinking about her. She knew. There was an animal intelligence in her eyes. He noticed this because the first thing she did on entering the Ultramar's back room was pay attention to the little owl. And when they sat down, on opening her notebook the first words she wrote, as he could see upside down, were 'little owl'. The blinds were half lowered and filtered a staircase of light. Mariscal had lit a Havana cigar, the smoke of which rose in rings that lazily came back to ground. He soon saw that extended periods of silence made her nervous, and this discomfort on her part made him feel secure. The animal's eyes were intelligent, but also meek. He liked this. He didn't have time for high voltage.

'What I mean,' continued the journalist, 'is that you got to where you are through your own efforts.'

'*Sensu stricto*, miss.'

'Lucía. Lucía Santiso.'

Good, Lucía, good. He felt at ease. He puffed out his chest and came out with one of his favourite quotations: 'A man's gotta do what a man's gotta do.'

'Do you also speak English?'

'I speak lots of languages. I'm a troglodyte.'

He let out a guffaw. He had no problem laughing at himself.

'The sea brings everything. Languages float as well. You just have to have a good ear. What do you think of John Wayne?'

The girl smiled. She'd end up being the one interviewed.

'He's from another time. *The Man Who Shot Liberty Valance*. I liked him in that.'

'A man is a man,' replied Mariscal transcendentally. 'That doesn't belong to another time, miss. That is intemporal. Cinema began with Westerns. And will go to hell, is already going to hell, when there are no more Westerns. It's the decline of the classic genres. Write that down.'

'I will do,' she said agreeably. 'We were saying you were a self-made man.'

'Let's just say I learned how to ride out the storm in my own dinghy. Without fear, but with common sense. You have to pray, yes, but never let go of the helm. What was it that sank the *Titanic*? A blasted lump of ice? No, it was the pace of greed, a loss of perspective. Man yearns to be God, but he's just . . . a worm. That's right, a drunken worm who thinks he's in control of the hook.'

'Mr Mariscal, people say . . .'

Mariscal pointed with his cigar at the journalist's notebook. 'Did you write down that bit about God and the worm?'

Lucía Santiso nodded uneasily. She knew the interview had been agreed between the editor-in-chief of the *Gazeta* and the lawyer Mendoza. There were a few ground rules. But Mariscal was growing far too much, his head, eyes, arms, everything, while she felt diminished.

'Mr Mariscal, your name is often bandied about as that of future mayor and possibly even senator.'

Mariscal joked, making out he was on stage: 'Ladies and gentlemen, before I speak, I would like to say a few words . . .' He didn't carry on until the journalist had let out a convincing laugh.

'Listen, Lucía . . . Can I call you that? Yes, good. I'm a dried fig by now, I'm not a danger to women,' and as he said this, he winked at her. 'Though dangerous women still get me going. Once a gallant, always a gallant. Don't write that down.'

Lucía lifted her biro off the paper. She was beginning to have fun and to calm down in time to the boss's baton.

'Listen, Lucía, I'm not going to lie to you. Politicians eat shit. Did you write that down? Yes? Then don't. That's right, I am apolitical. Absolutely apolitical. Ab-so-lu-te-ly! But put this as well. I, Mariscal, am prepared to sacrifice myself for Noitía.'

He waited for his words to have an effect, but the journalist continued writing in her notebook.

'To sacrifice myself and to fight for freedom!'

Mariscal accompanied this strong statement by banging his fist on the table.

This time Lucía Santiso did look up, forced to do so by the power of his rhetoric. She found herself face to face with a Mariscal transfigured. Looking serious, with flashing eyes.

'Freedom! You may think I don't go in for such a word . . .'

'Why would I think that?'

'Well, I do. I love freedom! Much more than those leeches who are always sucking on it. Freedom, yes, to create wealth. Freedom to earn a living with our own two hands. As we have always done!'

The cigar was forming low clouds, and for the first time Lucía Santiso decided to break a taboo. She looked down at Mariscal's hands.

He understood. He never spoke about this matter, but thought he would make an exception for this girl who listened and wrote with such intelligent meekness.

'Aren't you going to ask me why?'

'Why what?'

166

'Why I wear gloves.'

The editor-in-chief had already briefed her on this and had been strangely emphatic. 'He always wears white gloves. Don't even think about asking him about the gloves. It would seem he burned his hands while trying to rescue some money from the engine of a tanker. The tanker caught fire. He was taking emigrants to France. It was a miracle they got out.'

Lucía lifted her biro in a gesture of confidence. 'There's a journalist at the *Gazeta* who's allergic to touching door handles, phone receivers . . . And typewriter keys.'

'That's the one who'll be in charge!' said Mariscal, finally getting the journalist from the *Gazeta de Noitía* to laugh out loud.

'Don't worry. I won't mention your clothing. Just say you dress like a gentleman.'

'Then you'll be telling the truth. But I want you to ask about the gloves. There are all sorts of rumours, idiotic comments. All of it nonsense.'

'Why then? Why do you wear them?'

'I'll tell you the truth. I've never told anyone before. Because I swore to my dying mother I would never again touch a glass of alcohol. That's a real scoop now, isn't it?'

Lucía thought this might be a good moment to ask about something that interested her both professionally and personally.

'How did you make your fortune, Mr Mariscal?'

'With culture, basically.'

'With culture?'

'Yes, with culture! The cinema, the dance hall . . . I brought the classics. Juanito Valderrama, for example, singing "El emigrante"! Everybody cried. Now that's how you show you're a classic. Of course nobody remembers that any more. My motto was always the same as Metro-Goldwyn-Mayer's: *Ars gratia artis*. We even set the benchmark for hamburgers, way before McDonald's. Ours were better, of course. Nobody gave me anything, miss. But I'm going to let you in on a secret. I have always, always believed in Noitía. Noitía is an endless work in progress. It's fashionable nowadays to preserve the environment. Yes, that's fine. But what do we eat? The environment? . . . Did you include that bit about eating the environment?'

'It's a good metaphor.'

'It's not a metaphor!' exclaimed Mariscal, trying to stifle his cough. 'I already said I was apolitical. There are two kinds of politicians. Those who are off their heads. And those who walk about in water, asking for water. I'm not here to sing carols.'

The journalist decided to broach a sensitive subject in the gentlest tone possible.

'Which party will you stand for, Mr Mariscal?'

'I'll tell you. The one that's going to win!'

She understood his jokes. Mariscal accompanied the journalist's smile with a pleasurable exhalation of smoke. He felt jolly.

'Listen, the only party I'll stand for is Noitía. I like our way of life. Our religion, family, constant partying . . . If that bothers somebody, well, that's their problem.'

'But in Noitía strange things are happening. Do you approve of smuggling, Mr Mariscal? They say drug trafficking is spreading its nets here.'

Mariscal paused, never once taking his eyes off the journalist. There was an absolute silence in the Ultramar at that time, interrupted only by the fleeting sound of suppliers. The bakery van. The beer lorry. And so on. But now the Mental Department of Bothersome Sounds was reached by the voice of this journalist criticising the ever-increasing power of drug traffickers in Noitía.

Another Muhammad Ali. With a butterfly's wings and a bee's sting. *Biff!*

'Nets? Did you know that you'll have a better catch if a hunchbacked woman goes on board and pisses on your nets? Yes, yes. That's a fact and the rest is myth. Write that down. That is information. Listen, Miss Santiso, I don't go around complaining, asking, "What kind of shitty town is this?" Are we in the back of beyond? Well, no. *Velis nolis.* I like this place just as it is. I even like the flies here. You can tell we're prospering because we have a magnificent police station! And supposing, just supposing, there were smugglers in Noitía. Smugglers are honourable people. Those in Noitía anyway! Who are they hurting? The Inland Revenue? Listen, miss, if there weren't umbrellas, there wouldn't be banks.'

'I'm not sure I see the connection.'

'In the summer, banks lend umbrellas. When it rains, they ask for them back. Then there are people who make fantastic umbrellas for themselves. And the banks show interest. The Inland Revenue shows interest. In their own way everybody shows interest. Do you get me?'

'You haven't said anything about drug trafficking.'

'Did you write down that bit about umbrellas? Good. Listen, if I become mayor one day, I'll put an end to drugs. And drug addicts. I'll send them all to cut stone in quarries! There's a lot of talk about organised crime. Organised crime here, organised crime there. Your newspaper recently talked about organised crime in Noitía. What I'm saying is there are barefoot dogs everywhere. If crime is organised, then the state has to be better organised. And that's something we all have to contribute to. *Ipso facto.*'

Víctor Rumbo showed his face through the swing doors.

Mariscal glanced at him and gestured to him to wait. Then he gazed at Lucía's notebook, her calligraphic scrawl. He was about to make some comment about her fingers and nail varnish, something to do with crustaceans, but his tongue got caught in the only gap in his teeth. He looked at his watch.

'Did you write that down? About organised crime?'

'Yes, of course. It's a good thesis.'

'Well, now I want you to record the most important bit.'

A change overcame the whole of Mariscal. His expression. His voice. He gave weight to this organic transformation by rising to his feet.

'Of course if the first part isn't true, then the rest isn't either. The ancients used to say: *Modus tollendo tollens*. The way that denies by denying. I always rely on the ancients. They never make a mistake. There are no mafias in Noitía, miss. That's a myth. There may be the odd bit of smuggling. As always. As everywhere. But that's all.'

He said this out loud so that Brinco could hear. See how he was controlling the situation. Keeping a tight rein on the conversation.

Full stop.

Finis certaminis.

'That's the first interview I've given,' said Mariscal afterwards. He seemed satisfied with the experience. He became less formal with the journalist. 'I hope it's not your last . . . Include a bit of criticism, why not? The best way to sink somebody in the shit is by praising them to the skies!'

He turned towards the swing doors. Brinco gazed at them obliquely.

'Come in, son!'

Víctor Rumbo entered like someone clearing his way through a current of air.

'You're . . . aren't you . . . ?'

'I'm nobody,' Brinco interrupted her.

Lucía felt the violence contained in his voice. Took shelter behind Mariscal's presence.

'Would you permit me a photograph, sir? I don't know where that photographer's got to. He hasn't arrived yet.'

The Old Man glanced over at his new captain. He knew him well. He recognised the surge in his breathing, the wake of a confrontation.

'There was a man outside,' said Brinco suddenly. 'Taking photographs of the cars. I don't like people taking photographs of cars.'

'And what happened?' asked Mariscal uneasily. 'Did you send him to hospital for taking snaps of a few vehicles?'

'No. He'll just have to buy a new camera, that's all.'

Mariscal looked at Lucía and made a gesture of patience and apology with his arms. Agreed to have his photograph taken with the journalist's own camera. A way of making up for the damage.

'Go ahead!' he said finally. 'An old gallant can be persuaded to do anything!'

The boss positioned the brim of his hat, then crossed his arms with confidence, allowing the metal handle of his cane to appear next to the pocket silk handkerchief. Wrought silver with a pheasant's head.

'That cane is a beauty, Mr Mariscal.'

'The silver is silver, my girl, and the wood is from Itín. Always getting harder.'

His face seemed to harden as well, with carved features, as if offering a natural resistance to the succession of flashes.

'Is that it? If all goes well, you'll sell every copy. It'll be a great day for the *Gazeta*!'

'And if it doesn't go well?' asked Víctor Rumbo. This time he looked past her face. Lucía Santiso felt invaded by the piercing gaze of someone commonly known as Brinco, who now addressed her directly. 'If you wait outside, I'll tell you who nobody is.'

She hesitated. Said, 'I've a lot of work.' And then, 'I'll wait.'

Carburo got out of the van and approached the newspaper seller in the kiosk on Camelio Branco Square in Noitía.

'The *Gazeta*,' he growled.

This was his way of asking for things. The newspaper woman realised this and handed him a copy.

'No, no, I want them all.'

Now she did look at him in surprise. But this being the Ultramar, she was used to not sticking her nose in. She handed him all the copies. Finally let out, 'Has it got your obituary or something?'

Carburo pointed at the front page, with a picture of Mariscal. 'The boss is in it.'

His portrait occupied the centre of the page. His hat and white suit gave him the appearance of a dandy, which was re-inforced by the way he grasped his cane in the middle, lifting the handle to the height of his chest.

'Yes, I saw. He looks very smart,' said the kiosk woman with a hint of irony. 'Obviously he's the one who wields the stick. Why don't you take some flowers, Carburo? They're my last ones.'

The giant stared at the roses. 'No, I'm not hungry.'

He has a sense of humour, thought the woman. Only when he imitates himself.

34

'The Old Man is sorry.'

Víctor Rumbo got up from the rock where they were sitting next to Cons lighthouse, by the crosses in memory of dead sailors, and chucked a stone in the water. Turned around and stared at Fins. 'Sorry he's been so good to you.'

'What did he think? That I was going to come and buy some dynamite from him?'

'See what a troublemaker you are? The Old Man's right. Why is it so hard for you to be more pleasant? More . . . honest?'

'Honest? What do you mean?'

'Set your price. That would be the honest thing to do.'

'What's your price? Help me. Get yourself out of this web as soon as you can. It's not going to last for ever, Brinco. The judicial system will work, sooner or later.'

'You're dumb. Don't refuse my offer. I'm not going to be a grass. An informer. You know why? For one simple reason. There's more money on this side. The Old Man said, "Go talk to him, I'm still not sure if he's dumb or not." And I asked him, "How will I know, Mariscal?" He said, "If he burns any money, then he's dumb." How much do they give for a dead policeman, Fins? A medal perhaps. And a couple of lines in the newspaper.'

'Sometimes they don't even get that.'

173

'Do you want medals? We'll buy you some medals. Do you want to appear in the newspaper? Better to do it when you're alive than when you're dead.'

'Yes, it's always a bit more lively.'

They laughed together for the first time.

'Then you could devote yourself full time to your artistic photography . . .'

As he was making this suggestion, Víctor Rumbo pulled a couple of photographs from the inside pocket of his jacket. Handed one to Fins.

'As you see, we have people we can trust in all places. This is one you took of me in Porto airport with Mendoza. An interesting trip, as I'm sure you heard.'

'Yes, I heard something about it,' confirmed Fins, suppressing his surprise. Without further ado, he stretched out his hand for Víctor to give him another image. Brinco toyed with the photograph, using it to make the arching movement of an airship.

'This isn't one of yours!'

Fins examined every corner of the photographic paper. Tried to ascertain if it was a montage. He was amazed. It showed Brinco with the Colombian drug lord Pablo Escobar. Both of them laughing.

'Yes, yes . . . that's right! No, you're not hallucinating. With Pablo Escobar, on the Naples estate between Medellín and Bogotá. You should have seen the zoo. He had elephants, hippopotamuses, giraffes, lakes with black-necked swans . . . But the thing he liked best was cars. That day he was over the moon. His wife had just bought him a car driven by James Bond. He showed me another car that had belonged to Bonnie and Clyde . . . No, there's no trick. It's authentic. A real treasure, right?'

He stretched out his hand for Fins to return it.

'How much do you think it's worth . . . was worth?'

Brinco pulled out a lighter and set the image on fire. Let it burn to cinders. Then handed Fins the third and final photograph.

'This is the tops! A work of art.'

It was one of the photos Fins had taken from the docks, showing Leda in the window with a look of pleasure and Víctor embracing her from behind.

'Keep it . . .'

He stood up. Threw another stone into the sea. Headed back to the car, which was parked on the track leading to the lighthouse, but first turned around.

'The day you know your price, write it on the back.'

'How did it go?'

Mariscal was waiting for him in the back room of the Ultramar.

'He's turned ugly and there's no changing him,' replied Brinco.

The Old Man was about to say something, but interrupted it with a cough. He had this ability. He realised when something was inappropriate and stopped himself in time by drowning it in his throat.

'His father . . . Did he ask you about his father?'

'No, we didn't discuss the old days.'

'Better like that,' said the Old Man, standing up, swinging his cane, gazing at the little owl. '*Mutatis mutandis*, what do you know about his companion, that busybody who helps him?'

'She's another one. Doesn't stop digging around. She's not afraid of anything.'

'There's always something.'

'Well, she has a cat. I didn't know there were police cats!'

Brinco had used a touch of irony and the Old Man appreciated his effort.

'Once, in the cinema, somebody launched a cat from the top balcony. The Madman of Antas probably. He ruined the film. You've no idea how difficult it is to catch a good cat.'

35

A map of the world with pinned notes: tax haven, offshore, mother port, supply ship, transfer, unloading, consignment . . . The lines of routes and journeys indicated in different colours. The black line shows tobacco, the yellow line videotapes, and a third line, in red, cocaine. A green line, the transfer of personnel. One of these shows the following stages: Porto–Río–Bogotá–Medellín–Mexico–Panama–Miami–Madrid, with the initials VR–OM: Víctor Rumbo–Óscar Mendoza. In another section, photographs have been affixed using pins with different-coloured heads. There are more notes and Post-its placed according to their colour in such a way that they create a certain symmetry. The chart is like a kind of family tree, with the following label at the top: 'Limited Company'. The section devoted to personnel is headed by photographs of Mariscal Brancana, Macro Gamboa, Delmiro Oliveira and Tonino Montiglio, with several other, unidentified silhouettes. Lower down are Óscar Mendoza, with a question mark between brackets, and Víctor Rumbo. They appear as a hub from which there are connections to different places. One of the larger ones: Círculo Ltd, with dozens of photographs. One of the many secondary portraits shows Leda Hortas framed in the spy's window, and another one, Chelín Balboa, who seems to be smiling at the camera. A third section, denominated 'Grey Area', shows establishments, properties and businesses that act as fronts or laundries. Last of all is a chart called 'Shady Area', with branches leading to courts, security forces, communications, customs and banks. Here, like a kind of epigraph, are not specific notes, but codified numbers.

The map, photos, pins, coloured stickers, the different sections, all indicate a craftsman's patient hand and give the small workroom the appearance of a classroom. This is the space used hour after hour by Sub-inspector Mara Doval. Even though she's younger than he is and one of the first women in the body of investigators, Fins refers to her in private as Mnemosyne or The Professor. Tall and spindly. Long curly hair, a nest for the wind. She's making the most of her solitude and working barefoot at the moment. Wondering where to place the photograph of Dead Man's Hand.

When she hears the door groan, her first reaction is to find her sandals and put them on. When she lifts her eyes, she comes across the familiar faces of Fins Malpica and Superintendent Carro. And a third, unfamiliar man in uniform. Her look registers the significance of badges and stripes. He can't help himself, even if only for a moment, gazing at her painted toenails.

'Mara Doval, sir.'

The lieutenant colonel puts on some glasses and slowly, geologically explores this world emerging from the darkness. His gaze begins and ends with those feet.

'All this work . . .'

'No, it wasn't just me.' Fins makes the most of this opportunity to laud her to the skies. 'The goddess of memory, sir. It's all in her head.'

She tries to stop him with the language of signs, but Fins

refuses to heed them. 'What's more, she's the only one around here who really speaks other languages.'

They sit down at a round table, in the middle of which is an Uher reel-to-reel tape recorder. Mara presses a button, and the tape plays the voices of two women. A phone call between Leda and Guadalupe. Mara mouths the words. She knows every single sentence that is coming. The constant references to Lima and Domingo.

'Please tell us, Fins, who is on the cast list,' says the super-intendent when they've finished listening.

'The one placing the call is Leda. Leda Hortas is in a relation-ship with Víctor Rumbo, known in Noitía as Brinco. A celebrated pilot of speedboats. He seems to be on standby at the moment, but everything indicates his power in the organisation has grown. Leda's role, at this point, is to keep an eye on the customs patrol boats. She's phoning a beauty salon. The other voice is that of Guadalupe, Mr Lima's wife. Lima, sir, is Tomás Brancana. To everyone in Noitía, Mariscal. The Old Man. The Boss. The Dean.'

'And Domingo? Who is Domingo?'

'Domingo is the name used to refer to the customs patrol boats.'

'Is that as far as we've got?'

Mara Doval stands up to consult something on one of the charts. She removes a photo. Places it on top of the table. But first replies to Alisal's question, 'One other thing, sir. They don't need a spy any more. They've hired a customs chief directly.'

'I imagine these are all hypotheses,' suggests Alisal.

'Listen,' says Fins. 'They're very careful, cover their tracks, but occasionally they let in a ray of light. Listen.'

He presses 'play'. Leda is taking her leave of Guadalupe in a less formal tone than usual, and says that this will be their last conversation.

'Why is that?' asks Guadalupe in surprise.

Leda is obviously feeling very happy. 'We're going to move. It's about time!'

'And what about Domingo?'

There is a short pause. Leda finally lets out a laugh. 'He won the lottery!'

'But Mr Lima never told me anything.'

There is another pause. Leda, more distant, 'You know you don't just say those things.' Then, 'Ciao. Farewell!' And she hangs up the phone.

'That's a beauty!' remarks Alisal. 'A real indiscretion.'

'A rarity, sir,' confirms Fins. 'They have very good connections at the phone company. They always know when they're going to be tapped. Here we were lucky. And very patient.'

'Lots of patience with that pedicure, right, Mara?' remarks the superintendent.

She nods.

'How do we know Lima is Mariscal?' asks the lieutenant colonel suddenly.

Fins Malpica stands up, unlocks a drawer in the filing cabinet and pulls out a folder. Inside, in transparent plastic sleeves, are several handwritten sheets of paper, some creased, torn and put back together.

'The boss's handwriting,' says Fins with satisfaction. 'He never places a call. Never shows himself where he doesn't have to. Measures every single step he takes. Lives like a hermit. But here is his hand giving orders. In this scribble is the Old Man's twisted mind. A treasure for graphology. At last!'

Lieutenant Colonel Alisal has come to check a report of corruption in the barracks of the Civil Guard. Superintendent

Freire was right. But with these new revelations, the expression on his face is now that of a shocked, confused man.

'What quantity of cocaine are we talking about? Our statistics say we've been keeping them under control . . .'

'Statistics, as someone said, are the first lie.'

Fins feels he is able to be precise only through irony. 'I believe some of them may even have been doctored by the hand of the organisation's foremost lawyer, Óscar Mendoza.'

Alisal is downcast. Their gazes follow Mara Doval when, having opened a second drawer, she returns with another surprise. This time it's a chess set. She places it on the table. The pieces are large, expertly made, and imitate medieval figures. The colours are striking. Red and white.

'Would you look at that?' exclaims Alisal. 'Just like the Lewis chessmen.'

'A fantastic imitation,' agrees Doval. 'For those in the know. Of course they're not made of walrus ivory. Do you play chess, sir?'

'There are few things I enjoy more,' says Alisal. 'Even on my own.'

'Me too. Without pieces.'

Mara Doval unscrews one of the pieces, a pawn in the shape of an obelisk.

'They think cocaine is just this . . .'

She turns the pawn upside down and a small pile of white dust falls on to one of the squares. She does the same with the bishop and the rook in the shape of a warrior. Till she reaches the king and queen.

'But in fact it's this and this and this . . .'

Suddenly she lifts the board, revealing a false bottom full of the drug.

'And this! All of it flour.'

'We're talking about tons of the stuff,' says Fins. 'Thousands of kilos of cocaine. Thousands of millions in profit. Snow, blow, stardust! They want to turn this coast into the largest landing stage in Europe. It may already be that.'

Mara Doval adds, 'They'll buy out people, territory . . . They'll buy out everything. That's magical capitalism for you!'

Alisal is deep in thought, his gaze fixed on the chess set.

'It's the institutions that worry me. A worm is just a worm. The problem arises when the worm rots the apples. Superintendent, it's time we had a comprehensive, definitive report. They can write it. And I'll make sure it gets to where it has to.'

'We've already written the odd report,' remarks Fins.

'This time will be different, I promise.' Lieutenant Colonel Alisal bangs his fist on the table. 'If it's up to me, there'll be tremors in Babylon!'

36

In a small bay next to Cons lighthouse, between the rocks, lay the body of Guadalupe. There were local police, Civil Guards and ambulance staff. They'd recovered the body from the inside of her car, which had left the road and fallen like a lead weight into the water. Mariscal was informed and soon arrived. He looked grief-stricken. An accident. A mistake. The light had blinded her. When the coroner arrived, he offered his condolences. Mariscal's eyes were red. He looked old. Found it difficult to talk. The occasional murmur, apparent delirium. '*Chaves da vida*.' 'That carmine letter box . . .' 'I'm not going, I'm not going.'

'As everyone knows, we spent some time apart. This wasn't something I wanted. I was very sorry about it. She had this problem with depression . . .'

He mentioned this when the doctor from the Red Cross came over to compare notes with the coroner. 'It must have been early in the morning. Judging by the corpse, I'd say she's been dead for six hours.'

'What condition is the body in?'

'There's nothing strange about it, sir. Not a scratch. Certainly no sign of violence. With what we've got, I'd say it was death by drowning.'

Mariscal talked to himself and to others.

'She loved walking barefoot along the beach, feeling the water tickling her feet. She couldn't bear to be a day without seeing the sea. It was in her veins. Ever since she was a girl, you know? . . . I'm sure you don't . . . she worked over there, on the shore, gathering shellfish, the sea up to her waist. And that is where she died.'

'I'm sorry, Mr Brancana, but given the circumstances we'll have to perform an autopsy. A forensic autopsy.'

He breathed in through his nostrils. An energetic, hoarse inhalation of air which distorted his face. A forensic autopsy. He glanced over at that woman, Malpica's colleague, madly taking photographs of the corpse.

'Of course, coroner. Everyone is here to do their duty.'

Mónica, who worked in Bellissima, arrived at the beauty salon at the usual hour. Guadalupe, the owner, was the one who usually opened up. She did so an hour earlier. There weren't normally customers, but she used this time to make calls, place orders, etc.

Mónica rang the bell again. She was surprised. She looked at her watch. Tried to peer in through the frosted glass of the door.

This had never happened before. If there was some kind of problem, Guadalupe always let her know.

Nothing.

She got ready to wait. Half an hour at least. Guadalupe didn't like being called at home. But if she didn't turn up, Mónica would have to call. She took a pack of cigarettes out of her handbag and lit one.

A strong-complexioned man crossed the street. In a black leather jacket. She knew who it was. Carburo. He growled some kind of greeting. Hello, girl.

'You know something? Guadalupe's not coming.'

'Not coming? Till when?'

'Till . . . I don't know. She's not coming.'

'I don't understand.'

'You don't have to understand. She's not here. She's gone. She won't be coming back. The beauty salon's closed. Got it now?'

Mónica managed to unhook a cloud of smoke from her mouth.

She watched Carburo pull an envelope out of his jacket pocket, which he slapped against the palm of his hand in a gesture that was as meaningful as it was redundant, the way you would a wad of notes.

'Take this. It's a message for you. A very valuable one. Fifty thousand pesetas. Listen, Mónica . . .'

The girl stuffed the envelope into her bag as quickly as possible. She was afraid.

'While you were here, you saw nothing, heard nothing. You remember nothing. Am I right?'

She was incapable of answering. Not even a monosyllable. She shook her head in a panic. No, no, no.

'Good. Now the best thing for you to do is go. Far away from here, understand?'

'Far away?'

'Yes, far away. The further the better. And don't wait until tomorrow. Tomorrow is too late.'

As he said this, Carburo's gaze encompassed the surroundings, the insides of people passing by.

No, he couldn't believe it. She'd been the singer. Had had to wait twenty-five years like a dead cat.

He looked up at the sky. Too much light.

Is this how the devil repays the one who serves him? My very own prima donna!

The sinking was as a result of the height.

And that snotty-nosed Malpica calling me 'capo'. An idiot, a troublemaker, who thinks he's going to sort out the world.

Capo? He wasn't a capo. Like that other guy, who called him the head honcho. 'You're the head honcho, Don Mariscal.' He'd already warned him. 'There's no honcho around here, let alone a head one.' Aliases like that gave you away, made you look ridiculous. He could see himself on the front page of the *Gazeta*, 'Tomás Brancana the Head Honcho'. Then he thought about who he was. Gazed at the horizon, searched for the bell tower of St Mary's. He was . . . What was he? A dean. The Dean. That's right. There were priests in different parishes, and then there was the dean. No, the director of the seminary hadn't liked him. Because let's stop beating about the bush. The director knew what he'd said, and nobody else. He wasn't going to spill the beans. 'Are you sure about your vocation?' the director had asked. 'Yes, father.' 'How do you think you can serve God?' And here he'd noticed a touch of irony. Keep calm. The storm clouds are coming. As a child, ringing the bell of St Barbara's. No, he'd never said anything about becoming pope. Or bishop. Or even dean. 'The way God chooses.' 'But there must be something in your head?' 'A good parish.' This is what he'd heard as an acolyte in the sacristy, what one priest had said to another: 'Listen, Bernal, parishes are measured by the number of hosts that are consumed and the number of pesetas they bring in.' Neither pope nor dean. 'What I want is a good parish, father.' That's what he'd said. And who doesn't?

Mutatis mutandis.

Who'd have thought she would be the principal singer. The prima donna!

Floating like a butterfly, stinging like a bee.

Cassius Clay, aka Muhammad Ali.

The butterfly and the bee.

A good epitaph for Guadalupe.

37

His fingers tried to keep up with his thoughts, but couldn't. They galloped over the keys but sometimes had to go back, and then he would click his tongue in annoyance. He only stopped when he heard her mocking voice: 'Go for it, Simenon!'

'I lack the gift he had for writing and fucking at the same time, I'm sorry.'

'One has to appreciate one's limits. Take it easy.'

Mara's bare feet lay on top of the keyboard of her typewriter. The nails painted midnight blue. One of the last jobs in Bellissima. His colleague's gaze didn't exactly encourage an erotic game.

'Do you see something?'

In her lap were photographs of Guadalupe Brancana taken on the beach and the autopsy table.

'I see the face of someone who was afraid before she died. Very afraid. Long before she died. Years, perhaps . . . But I don't think that will be any use to the coroner or for the forensic report. It's artistic criticism, nothing more.'

'There are no skid marks on the road. Did you talk to the coroner?'

'He behaved very well. Whatever we may think, there's no way of connecting Mariscal to this death. And the girl, Mónica, has gone to ground. The fact is, Guadalupe was taking tranquillisers, which confirms the hypothesis of driver error. There are witnesses who saw her make several mistakes while out driving. They had no further consequences. Until yesterday, that is. In the end, though, barbiturates may have been her only source of affection.'

'I'm amazed. It's impressive working with someone who did their thesis on post-mortem expressions.'

'The head of department suggested I do it on *post-mortem auctoris*. The duration of authors' rights after their death. These are the legal cases of the future. Especially once the world has succumbed to those clever little machines that will do away with paper. But I wanted to compete with Darwin, who wrote on *The Expression of the Emotions in Man and Animals*.'

Mara placed her feet on the floor, leaned her elbow on the table thoughtfully and stared at Fins.

'You're doing all right yourself. Though the nickname Simenon wasn't my idea. I'm a fan of Hammett. They say you wrote a report that resembles a novel. A good novel at that.'

'If you want to screw a novel, say something nice about it. They'll bury the report, Mara, you'll see.'

'Well, I liked it. "Most excellent sirs: real power in Noitía is being exercised in darkness and silence . . ." Good opening. Sounds like an anarchist skit.' She then continued with the voice of a distant radio presenter: '"The only way to take effective action against organised crime is by seeing and listening in that zone of shadow and silence."'

As he listened to her in surprise, it occurred to Fins that the voice of truth had a hankering for fiction.

'I was just thinking . . .'

The one who opened the door, without knocking as usual, was Grimaldo, an overweight veteran inspector with fishy eyes and a sharp tongue. He was dressed like a careless dandy, carrying a copy of the *Gazeta de Noitía* which he threw on the table in front of Fins to reveal the front page.

There was a picture of Mariscal smiling and the following large headline:

Brancana, favourite for mayor
'NOITÍA WILL BE A MODEL OF PROGRESS'

Underneath the photograph, the subheading: *'In these parts, smugglers are honourable people.'*

Grimaldo was obviously in his element.

'Now there's a work of art to add to your chart on the Last Judgement. "Smugglers are honourable people." With a pair of balls! Don't let it get you down, Fins, enjoy yourself! Old Mariscal is quite the comedian. Check out this other pearl.'

ÓSCAR MENDOZA
NEW PRESIDENT OF THE CHAMBER OF
COMMERCE

'As with miracles, there are not two, but three. Let's have a look at the sports page. Allow me . . .'

With Víctor Rumbo as President
SPORTING NOITÍA ON A TOUR OF AMERICA

'Now isn't that wonderful? A team in the third division out to conquer the world! And captain of the expedition is their new manager, Chelín, a friend of all things pharmaceutical. I'm off. You can carry on slaving away for the Apocalypse. At dawn the moon will be eclipsed by a flight of hens! You'll be able to watch it from this tower, where the most secret confidential report on the ills of the world is currently being written. Not that there are many people left in Noitía who don't know about it.'

Micho Grimaldo left, scattering the sheets of newspaper in a triumphant cynical wake. Fins raised his middle finger. 'Go fuck yourself, Grimaldo!'

'I wouldn't bother,' said Mara. 'Don't waste your time with that sack of poison.'

'He should write the report. You know why? Because he's in on the secret.'

They were reading the section of social news in Noitía as a kind of collective obituary. Now somebody did knock at the door. Mara opened it.

'Fins!'

In came Lieutenant Colonel Alisal and Superintendent Carro. Their appearance wasn't exactly that of retreating superior officers being overwhelmed by a wave of corruption. The superintendent took the initiative with an effusive metaphor. 'We've been given the green light!'

'Tonight we'll put in practice Operation Noitía,' informed Alisal. 'Apart from high command, you're the first to know. We only have time to wait for reinforcements that are *uncontaminated*.'

'The phone tapping, sir ... That always puts paid to everything.'

'Don't worry,' said Alisal. 'We've cut all ears and tongues. Stuffed poison inside the molehills.'

38

'You frighten the balls, Carburo. That's why you win.'

Mariscal took amusement from the intimidating way in which his bodyguard played billiards. Carburo arched his body and, with the cue and his gaze in threatening symmetry, seemed to be giving the balls unappealable messages.

The phone rang.

The Old Man gestured with disinterest. Let it ring. He didn't like the way new technology stuck its nose in. Deep down the Portuguese Delmiro Oliveira was right when he joked, 'Mariscal is one of those who believe the Yankees never landed on the moon.' It was a personal matter. TV and videos were putting an end to cinema. The smuggling of tapes was profitable, but no more than that. *Peccata minuta*. It was the same with dance halls, which had finally closed owing to what he called 'all that paraphernalia'. As for the ringing of the phone, this was for him the technical triumph of interference in private affairs. It was a personal matter. The phone had destroyed the cowboy's way of life and put paid to horses in cinema. Without horses, there were no centaurs in the desert. Or speedboats, as Rumbo used to say. Poor Rumbo. Always trying to sound ironic.

There were three successive rings, which cut off. And then a fourth ring which continued. Mariscal paid attention to the machine. Affixed to the wall, black in colour except for the white of its dial, it gazed at him with the animal melancholy of its panoptic eye.

Without waiting for orders, Carburo picked up.

'Whoever it is, tell them I'm not here,' said Mariscal, looking at the other animal, the desiccated little owl. Its electric eyes had stopped working some time before. He'd ordered them to be repaired on more than one occasion, but that was the power of technology for you, he thought angrily. The old owl's eyes were still not working.

'Understood,' said Carburo, adding, before Mariscal could make a sign, 'Greetings to Mr Viriathus.'

Mariscal looked serious. Murmured, 'Mr Viriathus, eh?'

'Tonight, boss.'

Mariscal's mind didn't need further information to weave together the threads. This was a coded message reserved for extreme circumstances. 'Let's go, Carburo. We have to cross the border before midnight.'

Carburo immediately pulled back the green felt covering the billiard table, lifted two planks and uncovered a hole with a suitcase, which he passed to Mariscal. Mariscal opened it and checked the contents. Documents and a weapon.

An Astra .38 special revolver.

The boss glanced at Carburo. Rotated the cylinder. Weighed the gun in the air. Smaller than his hand, but fierce in appearance. Strong wood, dark steel. Snub-nosed.

'Don't tell me it's small, Carburo! It's a whole world!'

The Stick Under Orders silently prepared his .357 Magnum.

Brinco and Leda were dining in a recently opened restaurant in the new marina. The Post-da-Mar. A novelty, nouvelle cuisine making ground in Noitía. They were sharing a table with a couple their age, but there was an obvious difference between them. In the way they moved and spoke. In their clothes as well. All four looked elegant, but the clothes and ornaments of the other couple still shone as if they'd just come out of the shop window. He'd been director of a bank branch in Noitía for the last six months, while she had just taken over a jewellery franchise, which she talked about with gleaming enthusiasm.

'Your lady of the shipwrecks looks pretty tonight,' said Mara.

Fins ignored her comment. He was worried about something. 'Who are the others?'

'On glossy paper?'

'Yes. Where did those creeps come from?'

'Mnemosyne on the line . . . He's Pablo Rocha. Director of the branch I told you about, with a sudden, unusual interest in transfers from Noitía to Panama and the Cayman Islands, passing through Liechtenstein and Jersey. A real phenomenon.'

'He hardly needed to go so far. He could have laundered the money right here. There's no place like home!'

'Tell her that. Estela Oza. Just opened a jewellery store without the need for a loan or anything. Penniless before. It's amazing what you can do.'

They were on the lookout. They'd followed Brinco's car to this restaurant. He'd been driving calmly. There obviously hadn't been leaks on this occasion. Things were going well. Midnight was the appointed time to act. Arrests would be carried out simultaneously to avoid possible escapes. Till then, the instructions were to avoid using the walkie-talkies. The smugglers had laser equipment. When they'd searched Tonino Montiglio's rented apartment, the place had resembled a telecommunications hub.

Mara stuck her bare feet on the dashboard. Wiggled her toes like puppets.

'That dark colour . . .'

'Storm blue.'

'They look like Argonauts.'

'What do?'

'Your toes.'

'Like Argonauts? They're not after gold.'

'I'm talking about the real creatures. Those that live in the sea. The ugliest animals in existence!'

'Well, that's nice!'

Mara pressed 'play' on the cassette recorder. Listened with an exaggerated expression of amazement. To Maria Callas.

'And this?'

'"Casta Diva", "La mamma morta", "Un bel dì vedremo" . . . It'll play until it breaks. If you find anything better in the universe, give me a tinkle.'

Fins put something in his mouth.

'What are you taking?'

'Garlic pearls.'

'Give me one.'

'They're not garlic pearls.'

'I don't mind, give me one. I like novelties.'

'No, you can't take this.'

'It's not acid, is it? A trip with Maria Callas in the background has to be glorious.'

'I have St Teresa's disease,' said Fins, in line with the humorous tone of their conversation. 'The *petit mal*.'

He waited. Realised she was chewing it over. The goddess Mnemosyne's Department of Lie Detection working overtime.

'You're talking about a kind of epilepsy,' she said eventually.

'Without seizures or anything. Old people called them "absences". Having absences. It's not an illness. More like a poetic property. A secret. I thought I'd got over it, but it returned.'

'More reason to give me one.'

'No.'

'Yes!' Mara stretched out her hand. 'You know? She also belonged to the club of barbiturates.'

'Who did?'

'Casta Diva.'

The two couples dining in the Post-da-Mar were engrossed in conversation. The communication was especially good between Víctor and the banker Rocha. Without being rude to Estela, Leda paid more attention to the men's conversation. She approved of it, she liked it, but couldn't help noticing Víctor's growing and passionate interest in business affairs.

'But do you really think there are buyers in this part of Noitía for an estate with hundreds of villas?'

'You bet. Multiply by three.'

'Multiply what by three?'

Pablo Rocha spread his arms in a gesture that encompassed the infinite. 'Everything!'

It was half an hour before midnight.

A waiter came to the table and placed a leather folder next to Brinco. The folder with the bill.

'Mr Rumbo, if you wouldn't mind . . .'

Brinco was taken aback. He hadn't asked for the bill yet. He knew the waiter. They'd spent some time at sea together. Pepe Rosende. He was about to call him to order. Give him a ticking-off. But it was better not to create a scandal in front of the others. He opened the folder.

There was no bill. There was the restaurant's business card. He turned it over and read surreptitiously, with the folder half open. On the back, a handwritten message in the International

Code of Signals: *Victor India Romeo India Alfa Tango Hotel Uniform Sierra*.

Maintaining his composure, Brinco turned to Leda, 'Don't forget we have to make a call to Viriathus. Without fail. Before midnight.' Then to the other couple, 'Well, that was lucky! It's on the house.'

Leda stood up and took her handbag.

'Please excuse me, I have to visit the ladies' room.'

Brinco followed her. The other couple seemed mildly surprised, but carried on smiling.

'What are you thinking? I'm going to the gents, eh?'

The Post-da-Mar's emergency exit gave on to a small alleyway illuminated by tired lamps. Leda was waiting in the middle of the street with the car running. She didn't realise that Fins and Mara had followed her there and were hiding behind a parked car. 'It's the Nuova Giulietta,' whispered Mara. Brinco was about to get in the car when Fins floored him. Mara backed him up, aiming her revolver.

'Let go of me, you bastard! You've never grown up. You stink of shit!'

Fins forced him on to his front and managed to handcuff him.

'You've been living on borrowed time ever since you came back here,' muttered Brinco. 'But I swear this time I'll get you. Who the fuck do you think you are?'

'I see you still have a few coffins . . .'

'The Old Man was right. We should have packed you off to Chacarita cemetery as soon as you arrived.'

Leda suddenly opened the car door. Leaned out and shouted, 'Let go of him, Fins! Is this why you came back, you idiot?'

Mara now aimed her revolver at the voice that was speaking. Walked slowly towards Leda.

'What do you want? Don't tell me you're going to shoot. Fins, how good is this whore at target practice?'

'Much better than me!'

'We'll see . . .'

'Get out of here, Leda!' shouted Brinco, giving orders.

Mara was very close to her now. She stared in quiet surprise at the other's bare feet, the iridescent colour of her nail varnish. But unable to take any other decision, even to shout 'halt', she allowed Leda to lean back in, put the car in reverse, turn and accelerate noisily out of the alley.

Mara lowered her weapon. She was mute, downcast, like the lamps illuminating the street. She bent down and picked something off the ground. Leda Hortas' high heels.

After the bulletin's signature tune, the presenter read two news items. One referred to international politics and the other to Spanish politics. Then something about the economy, referring to the rise in petrol prices. Finally he mentioned the name of Noitía, and Mariscal let out a cloud of smoke.

'A total of thirty-six people were arrested last night and early this morning accused of belonging to drug trafficking and smuggling rings during the so-called Operation Noitía. Among the detainees was Víctor Rumbo, president of Sporting Noitía, alleged to be at the front of a powerful organisation. The operation, in which all the different security forces took part, was conducted with the utmost secrecy. As a result of numerous checks and inspections, huge amounts of drugs, cash and firearms have been confiscated.

'We will now hear from one of those responsible for the

operation, Lieutenant Colonel Alisal. "This was a harsh blow to the smugglers of tobacco. And also a way of stopping any kind of illegal trafficking. It sends out much more than a clear warning. Society should feel calm and criminals uneasy. From now on, they should know we are going to root out any such activities.'"

'I told you you could watch Spanish television from here.'

'It's better than over there!'

It was early in the afternoon. Delmiro and Mariscal had just had lunch. They'd settled into the sofa in a room in Quinta da Velha Saudade to watch the news. At the end, the Old Man lit a cigar.

He exhaled and watched the smoke climb, entwine the chandelier like ivy.

He clicked his tongue. 'You should try one of these, Delmiro!'

The ocean down by the South Pole had been lifted up. Chelín was sitting cross-legged in the Antarctic. He gazed at the image of Lord Byron contemplating the freedom of Greece. The best friend he'd never had. Serene unease. He shut the tome and placed it on top of the other on the shelf. Opened the suitcase with his nest. His tools for shooting up. The syringe, rubber band, jar of distilled water, teaspoon, filters, lighter. And, most important of all, the little ball. He secured the spoon in the gap between the two volumes of *Civilisation*. This way he had the bowl in front of him, the crater in which to ferment the sphere. That's right. He still had enough heroin for a good fix. A fix in three movements. He had to pump in three movements. Pump the blood. A mouse stared at him from the middle of the ocean. He was used to them scurrying about. Used to the blind gaze of the mannequin, the gaze of the one-armed skeleton and the desiccated crane. But the mouse's gaze was enormous. It was far away, but touched him with the graphite of its eyes. A mouse contemplating the freedom of Greece.

The nest in his suitcase was a hole surrounded by wads of dollars. There was room for the pendulum and the Astra Llama. A treasure for the freedom of Greece. He'd have given anything for a kiss. A bit of saliva in his mouth.

Chelín put everything back under the ocean's planks.

Fins Malpica's first impulse was to sniff the air. It wasn't meant to be an overreaction. If he did this, it was because he felt truly dizzy, a dizziness that was accompanied by the smell of burning oil. He managed to control himself. Change his expression of disgust for one of total seriousness.

And this is how he emerged from the courthouse. Descending the stairs like someone counting the steps and finding that several are missing. There were people outside, a cluster of journalists, waiting to hear the sentence passed on Víctor Rumbo, the main detainee in Operation Noitía. Fins didn't answer any questions. He ignored the microphones. Gulped back the historic sentences.

'What happened, inspector?' asked a journalist.

'You'll hear about it soon enough.'

He was learning to talk like a cynic. He didn't avoid the cluster of hostile faces. Nor did he issue any challenges. He just walked on by like a man without a care in the world. Which is to say, a man who is fucked.

On his way to the car, he met Mara. She was distracted. Confused by the run of events.

'They're going to set him free. It's unbelievable,' said Fins. 'The bail's tiny. You'd have thought Rhesus Negative had lent a hand.'

'Rhesus Negative?'

'One of the court's henchmen.'

Leda Hortas pushed open the door of the courthouse and exclaimed happily, 'He's been set free!'

There was Brinco with his ace's smile, accompanied by two other important detainees, Inverno and Chumbo, and by the lawyer Óscar Mendoza. From the top of the stairs, the lawyer took control of the situation. 'Ladies and gentlemen, a good day for Noitía! My client, Víctor Rumbo, has been set free. Later on we'll give the details. The important thing now is to celebrate the fact that justice has been done and our beloved neighbour can come home. Thank you, everyone!'

'Mr Rumbo, how are you feeling?' asked the journalist Lucía Santiso.

'Better than those who arrested me. I slept very well in fact.'

He caressed Leda. Put his arm around her. Kissed her. The scene was reminiscent of a medal ceremony.

'And tonight I'm sure I'll sleep even better!'

In the car Mara suddenly asked Fins, 'What would you do if you got home and found your cat dead?'

'By "dead", do you mean really dead?'

'Yes, I mean they killed him. Killed him and hung him on the door handle. Just like in the old days.'

Fins placed his hands on the steering wheel. Didn't dare look at her. Or touch her.

'Can I put on Casta Diva?' she asked.

'Of course you can. It's there until it breaks.'

39

In the middle of the Vaudeville's stage was a Cadillac Eldorado. Víctor Rumbo had bought it in Cuba. Seen it in Miramar, contacted the owner and not stopped until, when Brinco said it was his last day on the island, the owner had gestured to him to get in the car and take it for a drive. 'Let's go for a *paseíto*!' He always told this story. And whenever he got mad, this was what he said, 'Let's go for a *paseíto*!' He was terrifying when he said it. Because the business with the Cadillac got complicated. When it was finally unloaded in Vigo, Brinco's expression changed. He spat out curses so foul they wounded the clouds. All that had arrived was the Eldorado's bodywork. It wasn't that he minded so much, despite all the administrative headaches. He only wanted the sedan for decoration. What bothered him was that the emblem on the bonnet was missing.

'Where's the lark? Where's the fucking skylark?'

The package had been sealed, they explained in customs. Encased in wood. This was how it had travelled. Víctor Rumbo was spewing smoke. In his rage he'd forgotten the owner's name. Called him 'Let's Go'. Shouted it out. Across the sea. A raving lunatic. 'Let's Go' and 'Skylark'.

'Don't get so upset over a steel bird,' commented Óscar Mendoza. 'I'll get you one from a Rolls-Royce. The Spirit of Ecstasy. Now there's an emblem!'

'You don't understand,' shouted Brinco. 'This one was mine. My own fucking skylark! I didn't know what it was. And that bastard went and told me it was a lark.'

So he sent Inverno to Havana with the details, Let's Go's address and the instructions, 'Don't come back until you've got the emblem.'

In the middle of the stage was the Cadillac with its emblem.

Víctor Rumbo wanted to turn the Vaudeville into something straight out of a film. A before and afterwards in Noitía's history. Till then, most singles clubs on coastal roads had been run-down, sinister places with depressing architecture oozing neon pus. The Vaudeville was going to be different. Unforgettable. A club that would cause stylish scandal among the jet set after a wild night out. Mendoza, Rocha and the increasingly active and enterprising Estela Oza were partners, with the corresponding front. For his part, Brinco wanted the Vaudeville to be an outrageous present for Leda. He went so far as to imagine her as the great madam reigning over her kingdom, controlling everything from an office with screens relaying what was going on in every corner. In the public and private rooms, but also in the bedrooms. She had character, ambition and style. Come on. She had more style, a savage attraction, than Estela Oza ever would. But things turned out otherwise. As expected, he did his bit. Went and found the women. Because this is how it works. People think prostitutes travel around like tourists. Well, no. You have to attend the auction. Check their teeth. Compete with other buyers. Tame them. Protect them. So to speak. This was Brinco's business. And he did what he had to. He bought the meat.

The inauguration was unbelievable. There were some surprising guests in attendance, some of the jet set, those Brinco knew looked the other way to avoid greeting him. And, above all, amazement, exclamations, when they entered the covered terrace with its large transparent column full of hummingbirds in suspended flight around the serpent of a bougainvillea flower. In the back room, where there was a place for playing cards, another exotic surprise that caused consternation among men and women. An aquarium in which warrior fish fought each other. Red dragons. A kind of host dressed in a shimmery satin jacket replaced the severed fish and sang the bets. On the main stage, with the Eldorado in the background, its bodywork glistening more than the host's satin, a show billed as the real Tropicana.

But in the midst of all this uproar something was missing. Brinco kept asking after Leda and eventually sent Inverno to fetch her from the Ultramar. She came. Apologised for being late. Domestic matters. Her arrival did not pass unnoticed, she had a genuine air of dangerous elegance, and Brinco lost the face of someone searching for a fallen tooth. One absence was mentioned, especially among the less well informed. Where was Mariscal? But neither Víctor nor his circle asked themselves this question. The Old Man didn't like large groups of people. He'd be floating around, with his panoptic eye, working out the moment when the void would demand his voice.

Leda would never come back to the Vaudeville. Brinco soon understood she avoided ever mentioning the subject. She'd decided it didn't exist. On him, however, the large blue neon sign, with its pink skylark blinking in an arc above the letters, had a hypnotic effect. It stood on the hill, visible from the whole valley, defying the dark and the sea.

The wave of high rollers soon washed away from the Vaudeville. Among the partners, only Mendoza the lawyer continued to visit.

He liked the girls and could fuck for free. That was the reason for his loyalty. Though there were more of them, the Vaudeville's customers ended up being the usual clientele of a singles club. Lads on a night out. Old men with money. And *flour* people. Especially those glorious days after a shipment.

'Who's that? Belvís? You're joking. Didn't he lose his mind or something?'

It was Belvís, the ventriloquist, the orchestra man, with his friend the Kid. Víctor Rumbo carried on organising programmes for the weekends. Not the spectacular stuff he'd done to begin with. Now the most frequent event was a lazy singer followed by an erotic act. But one day Belvís arrived. He got off the bus at Chafariz Cross with a suitcase. Brinco stopped the Alfa Romeo and told him to hop in. Belvís was happy, he'd always liked novelties.

'What happened to Charlie?' asked Brinco.

Belvís looked at him in surprise. To tell the truth, Belvís always looked in surprise. 'The Kid? The Kid's here, in my suitcase. He likes it better in Conxo. More people to talk to. But you have to get out a bit.'

That was when Brinco announced, in that solemn tone he had, 'Well, get ready. Tonight you're going to perform at the Vaudeville.'

Belvís entered the stage with his suitcase. Cast an admiring glance at the Eldorado. Not because he was acting, but because it struck him as a magnificent ship with a skylark on its lips. He opened the suitcase. Took out the Kid. Sat down on the stool. Looked out for the first time. Realised there was a lot of noise since most people weren't looking at him. At either of them. There was a long bar at the back where customers stood on their own, holding a glass. Checking out the terrain. With a hawk's eyes. Another group was talking and laughing out loud, completely oblivious to Belvís and the Kid's stellar presence. The only couples paying attention were those at the second row of tables, closest to the stage. Belvís searched for Brinco. He'd been there, in the corner, when he brought him in. Had introduced him to a girl with big eyes, whose name was Cora. He was searching for those big eyes in order to start looking around. But there was no one there. Neither Brinco nor Big Eyes. Only Inverno. The eternal lookout.

'Thank you for your indifference,' began Belvís. 'I'd like to introduce you all to Charlie the Kid. An intellectual.'

'Can I tell a story, Che?'

'Course you can, Charlie. It's what everyone expects . . . Just make sure you finish quickly. They're important people and haven't time to waste on your intelligence.'

'OK. The other day I overheard a conversation. You know I'm always overhearing conversations. It was right here in Noitía, or maybe not. The point is, one girl said to another, "Listen, I'm in a quandary. The judge said I could choose between a million pesetas and a year in prison." So the other said, "I don't know why you're even wondering. Take the money!"'

'People are amazing, Charlie. I remember a bar like this, full of lowlife . . .'

'Do you realise what you just said?'

'Have I offended somebody?' asked Belvís.

'Course you have! Apologise to the owner. This isn't a bar. It's a . . . club!'

'Pay attention to me, Charlie.'

'No, I'd prefer not to,' said the puppet, glancing at the ventriloquist and giving a jump. 'Your hand's enough. You won't let go of me!'

And that was when the Kid looked around, very slowly, at the audience finally beginning to laugh.

'Well, would you believe it? Look at them. Created in his image and likeness. Just imagine! That supreme being was a funny man. He must have been delighted!'

'That's right. Man was created in his own image and likeness. That's what the Bible says.'

The Kid searched around for someone special to look at. A guy with a classic grumpy face. Bushels of hair in each nostril serving as a moustache. Projecting eyebrows over a pair of rodent eyes. Each wrinkle resembling a scar. He clenched his teeth and seemed to growl. Next to him, wearing a serious expression, was a girl.

It was her the Kid addressed. 'Tell me, darling. What's it like to sit so close to God, the divine grace?'

The couple reacted well and laughed. But in the group at the back, who hadn't been paying much attention, there was a drunken scuffle. Inverno knew them. The first was Lelé Toén, one of Carburo's men. The other, Flores, nicknamed the Graduate. He'd been in Noitía for a couple of days. A Mexican guest of Macro Gamboa. He knew he should leave them alone. They'd soon grow tired.

But for some reason Flores decided this puppet had to stop talking. He started shouting, staring at the Kid, not Belvís. Calling him a son of a bitch, his bald mother, and so on. Inverno thought it might be time to call Brinco. He'd be busy with Big Eyes, but he'd better call him all the same.

'Calm down,' said Lelé to the Graduate. 'It's only a comedian with a puppet. A clown. A lunatic.'

'A lunatic? Nobody calls me a dirty pig.'

Stay quiet, thought Brinco at the other end of the bar.

But Belvís opened his mouth. 'Did you hear that, Charlie?'

'We were talking about God and someone changed the subject. Anyone got a ribbon to tie around a pig?'

The Graduate bent down and pulled a weapon from under his trousers, strapped to his calf. A change of subject. He aimed at the puppet and shot it in the head. Another shot rang out. Now the Graduate was moaning, the hand that was previously armed having been wounded.

'Go pluck this cock outside before the police turn up,' Brinco ordered Lelé.

'The boss won't like it.'

'Who cares? In the Vaudeville, I'm in charge.'

Belvís was holding the puppet in his lap. Caressing it. 'Can you hear me, Charlie? Can you hear me, lad?'

'You're lucky you weren't shot.'

Brinco picked up some fragments of wood from the ground.

'If the cops turn up, don't say anything. The mouth is for keeping quiet.'

40

'Now this is what I'd call a tax haven,' declared Óscar Mendoza as he arrived for the party. Everyone knew he was joking and being serious at the same time.

Romance Manor had access to the sea, as Leda had wanted, but also a brand-new swimming pool. The gate to the sea really did give way to an Eden. A cove of fine white sand with a gurgling brook creating its very own garden next to the dune-working wind. And an old stone embankment for mooring boats.

Víctor Rumbo clapped his hands to summon the guests in the garden. He was obviously excited and managed to thread together a discourse that was sealed by applause and laughter.

'As you know, the manor belongs to Leda. I'll have to make do with the bed . . . But for Santi there's something special. Come with me!'

He lifted his son in the air, sat him on his shoulders and directed the guests to where the surprise was waiting. There was a large open space covered by a blue canvas. Brinco gestured with his hand and a violinist began to play a waltz. Another gesture told some workers it was time to remove the cover since the guests were now surrounding the large rectangle.

There was the swimming pool. But it wasn't empty. Out of the depths emerged a dolphin. Followed by a murmur of appreciation. Brinco didn't need to gesture any more. Everybody fell into astonished silence while the violin bow arched over the cetacean's back.

'You wanted a friend? There's a friend for you!'

Chelín followed Leda with his gaze. Managed to attract her attention. Took the pendulum out of his pocket and placed it next to the ground. It began to swing. She nodded, laughing. It was true. Now she was the one leading her son around the swimming pool while a group of men, partners and friends, surrounded Brinco with their aperitifs.

'Brinco, your friends also have a surprise for you,' said the lawyer with more familiarity than usual. 'Come on then! There are marvels of nature for you too!'

The group headed towards the main gate, Mendoza and Rocha ushering them on.

'And Inverno? Where's Inverno?' asked Brinco.

The lawyer clapped his hands and the main gate opened. In came a limousine with tinted windows, moving at a snail's pace, followed by a group of mariachis with Inverno at the front playing the Mexican ballad 'Pero sigo siendo el rey'.

The doors of the limousine suddenly opened and out stepped three gorgeous girls in revealing evening dresses.

'Your Vaudeville princesses!'

They acknowledged the reception. Twirled around like models and then kissed Brinco.

Leda heard the music. Recognised Inverno's strong voice. Came to see what was happening. Santiago was playing with the other boys, so she went on her own. Or almost on her own. Chelín followed her at a short distance. Because he knew her, he realised she would turn around angrily as soon as she saw the limousine and the welcome given to the girls from the Vaudeville. And he was right. Leda spun around in a rage, rushed up the stairs leading to the terrace and first floor.

Chelín went after her. 'Wait. Where are you going?'

She eyed him like a stranger. Like someone who'd lost touch with reality. 'What do you care? To tart myself up!'

'Leda, you know I always brought you good luck.'

Good luck? She was about to carry on. Another lunatic. But she set her eyes on him. Recognised him. It had been ages since she'd felt so much like crying. She didn't cry. She stroked his cheek with her fingertips. He was very thin. A child's gaze with steel spikes on his chin.

'That's right, Chelín.'

'Remember when we used to hunt for treasures? I discovered something. I discovered there are only treasures under the ocean. That's where shipwrecked and dead people keep them. That's where you have to look for them. Under the ocean. Say "ocean", please.'

Leda listened to him with surprise and concern. There was something wrong with him. He wasn't well. He'd fallen again. There was nothing more unsettling than an unsettled gaze. She smiled, and he did the same. That worked. She placed her cheek against his. Concave–convex. That also worked. 'Ocean.' Then a kiss. A little peck. She turned on her heels and ran up the stairs.

'A little saliva,' he mumbled. 'How lucky I am!'

Brinco summoned Chelín. He was holding Cora, his favourite from the Vaudeville, by the hand. 'Now you're going to see the second thing I like best to do in the world. Where are the stars, Chelín?'

If it was meant to be a joke, he didn't understand. His mind was elsewhere. Stars? Oh, of course, what a fool! He ran to fetch the firework launcher. There they went. A sun, a palm tree and then a Bengal light that descended very slowly.

When Cora looked down from the sky, she blinked. She didn't want her eyes to cry. But her eyes had a will of their own. She could hide everything except for her eyes, God damn them.

'That's the most special present anyone's given me for a long, long time.'

Víctor went into the bedroom where Leda was. He was still in his party outfit, but she'd decided to put on silk pyjamas. She was seated in front of the dressing table, compulsively brushing her hair.

'What is it, girl? Everyone's asking after you. You suddenly disappeared.'

'How I wish I could disappear! You should have told me you were going to bring the whole harem to the house.'

'Leda, they're just employees who work at our clubs.'

'Employees? Our clubs? Don't talk to me like that!'

'What do you want me to call them? Whores? One whore here, another there. They're here because they want to be! Go and open the gates and tell them to leave. You'll see how many actually do.'

'Like dogs. Dogs won't leave either, Brinco. What do you take me for? You buy these girls like cattle. How much did you pay for that one?'

'Which one?'

'The one without a right toe.'

The toe. That blasted right toe. Why did they have to wear sandals? He'd already warned them. Don't dress like that, girl, you look like a slave. You make it look like I chopped it off with an axe.

'I didn't cut her, for fuck's sake. It was already cut.'

'Oh, I see. She was branded when you bought her. I'll take the amputee. Aren't you a good boy, Brinco, you son of a bitch?'

'All right, so I know a thing or two about prostitutes . . .'

Suddenly his rage boiled to the surface. She deserved a good hiding. He tore open a drawer, rummaged around and pulled out a leather-bound bible with a zip. *Holy Bible*. Nácar-Colunga BAC. He opened it, threw it on top of the bed. As the leaves fell apart, hundred-dollar bills floated down on top of the covers.

'A bible for each one. Do the sums.'

Leda couldn't come down. She was indisposed. Something she'd eaten. The same old story. That's right, something she'd eaten or drunk. She had to look after herself. Víctor Rumbo took his leave of all the guests. Some of them inebriated. Like Chelín. He was turning into a real pain.

'Brinco, you know I always, always brought you good luck.'

'Sure you did.'

'Always!'

'Always.'

Óscar Mendoza asked if he'd invited Mariscal. Of course he had. Why hadn't he come?

Brinco pointed to a hill in the night. Said, 'Look, Óscar. He'll be up there. Watching everything. Happy and solitary as a wolf.'

41

Various messages arrived from Mariscal. Nothing about Flores. If the Graduate couldn't look after himself, that was his problem. But there was something else. And this worried him. Mariscal wanted to see him in the Ultramar. Something was beginning to stink. What was beginning to stink? Money. When it came to money, Víctor Rumbo knew a stink meant only one thing. The lack of money.

'The payment's been made. I'm sure of it.'

'Milton's two-thirds? Don't be so sure. Who was the courier?'

An unfamiliar sweat appeared on his forehead, dripping into the caverns of his nose. He thought about it quickly. Didn't reply to Mariscal's question. Said, 'I'll check it out.'

'That's better.'

He talked to Chelín. It took him a while to call, but in the end he called. There'd been a complication. He'd been late for the meeting. He knew it was in Benavente. But everything was OK. Under control. He sounded confident. He'd organised a second meeting. Had all the coordinates. Everything was arranged. The payment would take place in Madrid. To make up for the inconvenience.

Brinco spent the following day in the Vaudeville. He was expecting a confirmation call that evening. That was what they'd agreed on. But the call came from Carburo. Nobody had turned up for the meeting in Madrid. Brinco set Inverno, Chumbo, everybody he had, in motion. He even spoke to Grimaldo. Find Chelín. No, he didn't want him to call. Bring him in. As quickly as possible. Whatever it took. By the balls if necessary.

But Chelín had gone to ground. A long time passed. Three days was far too long. The whole world could go crazy in under three days. And that was what was happening. The rumbles got louder and louder. Closer to home. And one of the loudest, this annoyed him, came from Óscar Mendoza.

He'd drunk too much. That night and the previous nights. To see if one hangover could cure another. He was leaving the Vaudeville with Cora. He'd come up with one of those stupid, wonderful ideas. To take her somewhere special.

OK, he hadn't drunk so much. He was OK. Yes, he felt better. Come on, you. Tonight is going to be special. He was just about to unlock his car when another ground to a halt. Out got Inverno, who opened the back door. Chumbo shoved Chelín outside.

'Here he is,' said Inverno. 'We caught him in Porto. About to board a plane.'

'We got a tip-off from a friend of Wiggy's,' added Chumbo.

'Where the hell were you going?' Brinco demanded of Chelín. Or rather of the half-man that had once been Chelín.

'To Greece.'

'To Greece? What the fuck were you going to do in Greece?'

'I always wanted to go to Greece, Brinco. You know that.'

A bag of bones. Since the last time he'd seen him, he'd lost a lot of weight. He was as thin as a flatfish. But the worst thing was his face. Those sunken eyes. Better calm down a bit.

'So where's the money, Chelín?'

'There's nothing left, Brinco. They played that trick with the aeroplane. Went and stole it. I thought it was them when it was someone else.'

'What are you trying to tell me, Chelín?'

'You have to help me, Brinco. They're after me. They're going to kill me!'

Víctor tore back the sleeve on his left arm. 'Oh, for fuck's sake! For the love of God! Hadn't you given this up, you prick?'

'Don't leave me, Brinco, don't leave me . . .'

The lights in a few windows had gone on. The first sign of complaints.

'No, I won't leave you. It's not your fault. Let's get out of here. Come on!'

Inverno pushed back the levers in the junction box to turn on the floodlights. The football pitch lit up. Chumbo took a throw-in. Víctor Rumbo was leading Chelín by the shoulder. Not violently, but holding on to him. They walked towards the nearest area. It was cold on that large open pitch and Cora waited behind, trying to warm herself up with her own embrace. The boss called to her, however. 'Come on, you.' And she obeyed, moving like a tightrope walker, her heels sinking into the grass.

'Don't fuck me, Brinco. What the hell are we doing here?'

'What do you think? We're going to play!'

He pushed Chelín into the goalmouth. As he was talking, he placed the ball on the penalty spot.

'We won a lot of matches together, remember? You were a fucking great goalie. OK, a good one. A guy I could trust. Isn't that right?'

In the middle of the goalmouth, Chelín looked disorientated, shipwrecked. But the position he was in helped him. He remembered the keeper he'd been. Stood tall. A little bit.

Brinco gave himself a run-up to take the penalty. But then suddenly turned to Cora.

'Why don't you take it?'

'I'm not sure I can.'

Cora took off her shoes.

'Oh, come on, Brinco! Don't let her take it.'

'Go on, girl.'

Cora ran barefoot and kicked the ball with all her might. Chelín tried to save it. A dive to one side, at the limit of his strength, which left him lying on the ground, moaning softly.

The others left. He saw them from where he was lying. With their backs to him. Cora's shoes, which she held in her hand. The only thing similar to a farewell.

He tried to get up, but his body preferred to remain on that bald patch of earth. His eyes were taken in by the leathery, indifferent line of grass, the goalkeeper's nightmare.

'I always brought you good luck. What do you think?'

Carburo cut a strange, solitary figure that night in the Ultramar. In a white apron, static as papier mâché, his arms crossed, an angry expression, rooted in front of the television. The map of isobars. There was a knock at the door. He used to like haranguing the weatherman. What had happened to the weatherman? Perhaps he was a fugitive and this was him at the door, seeking shelter.

There was another rap at the glass door. The beating of a tambourine. Carburo moved the curtain and saw it was Brinco. With merry company. Just what he needed. He opened up silently. He wasn't the kind to pretend he was pleased to see you.

'Evening, Captain Carburo! We've come to ride out the storm!'

'What storm?'

Brinco laughed. Carburo's permanent bad mood always struck him as funny. Having climbed the stairs, on the landing he embraced Cora around the waist from behind. They walked like this, swaying slightly, covered and uncovered by the curtains the wind puffed out.

'How well you ride the wind!'

When he saw the door of the suite, Brinco's expression changed suddenly. Became tense. Hardened. Looked back.

'Fucking wind! Why don't they ever shut the blasted windows?'

'What you looking at?'

'The sea!' Cora seemed moved, like someone who's found an image she's always dreamed of.

'The sea? Aren't you sick of looking at the sea?' Brinco went over to the window. 'Besides, you can hardly see it.'

She knew he was half drunk. She'd started to know him well. The other half filled sometimes with electrified passion, others with a sickly blackness. When he spat out his words, she didn't flinch.

'Yes, you can. It's on fire.'

'On fire, eh? That's good, girl. Stay where you are.'

She stayed. On the bed. Gazing through the window at a sea that could be seen and not seen. Víctor went into the bathroom and switched on the light, the door half open. He looked at himself in the mirror. This sweat. This unfamiliar sweat. He rinsed his face with cold water. And again. Looked at his wet face. Raised his fist to break the face that was now in the mirror. But in the end moved his fist aside and banged the wall. Had difficulty breathing, as after a long fight. His forehead pressed against the mirror. The freshness.

Cora came over to the door. Didn't push or look. Just whispered, 'Are you all right?'

'I'm fine!'

'Are you sure?'

'Every night I smash a mirror with my fist. It's a custom of mine . . .'

He glanced at her, and, used as she was to the tones of his voice, this time she couldn't say whether she was the witness or object of his hostility. Unsettled, she went back to the bed, to her side next to the window, and slowly began to undress.

Brinco came out of the bathroom and went to his side of the bed, in the half-shadows. He lay down in his clothes, face up.

Everything registered a mute silence. In a move that was in fact defensive, Cora went over to him, naked, not touching him, but curling up into a ball.

'The sea brought you as well, didn't it?'

'I don't know, I don't know . . .'

'The key!'

'He's got it,' said Carburo meekly. With this woman he only knew how to obey.

'The other key!'

All the wind piled up for years on the landing, like grass pressed inside a silo, was exploding. The nightmare was bursting inside her eyes and she flung open the door.

Brinco and Cora lay on the bed, both naked. Hearing the door creak meant sticking his hand under the pillow, in search of his weapon.

But he soon saw it was Leda.

Leda carrying something in her hand. One of those leather-bound bibles with a zip. Leda opened the bible and shook free the dollar bills that floated down on top of the bare bodies.

'What the hell are you doing?'

'I'm buying her. She's mine. She's free!' shouted Leda.

She grabbed Cora's arm and forced her to stand up. In the middle of all this uproar, Cora glanced at the sea, the ashen paste, the oily fringe of foam. As for the rest, scraps of evanescent mist.

Leda grabbed her shoulders. Shook her about. Talked to her violently of freedom. Freedom which for Cora had a double meaning. Was always used as a threat. She'd crossed borders, as a mule, with condoms stuffed full of money inside her vagina or her digestive tract. On the verge of exploding. Why not try to buy off this policeman? The way he looked at her was very like this woman shaking her. You don't know whether what they want is to set you free or hold on tighter. It was better not to try. The border policeman was in on the loop. Luckily she caught the gesture he made, the axial connection with the guy waiting at the checkpoint.

'You're free, understand? I don't want to see you round here ever again! Take that money and leave.'

Leda released the girl and from the doorway shouted at Víctor, who was getting dressed in an appearance of calm. Patience. The storm would soon pass.

'As for you, you bastard, go to the football pitch.'

She'd disappeared down the landing, swallowed up by eternal waves of curtain, when he finally registered what she'd said.

'What's that, Leda? Wait!'

There were ambulances and police cars parked at the main entrance to the football pitch, so he turned at the crossroads in

A de Meus, took the left fork along the coast as far as the mirador in Corveiro.

From there he could see the pitch. What under his presidency had been renamed the stadium the day they inaugurated the covered stand with its directors' box. From afar, it looked like a table-football table whose players had detached themselves from the metal bars and taken on a life of their own. In fact he didn't want to see. He grabbed the binoculars not to get closer, but to have something between his eyes and the other.

Chelín was hanging from the crossbar.

42

They stopped to have lunch at África's place. A small bar and shop on the corner between the coastal road and the track leading to the refrigerated warehouse. As soon as they entered the bar, even before she served the coffee, África signalled to Brinco to approach the counter. 'Some clients of yours arrived early. A jeep went up the track.'

'The same two as always?' asked Brinco ironically.

'No. They weren't guards, nor were they from around here.'

Brinco was grateful for the information. And knew how to pay for it. Inverno was driving the Land Rover and they were accompanied by Chumbo sitting in the back. When they reached the bend overlooking Cons, before they could see the warehouse built on reclaimed marshland, Brinco ordered Inverno to stop. Told Chumbo to get out.

'Go and check out the scenery.'

Chumbo didn't ask any questions. Just disappeared down a track between bushes, in the direction of the rocks.

When he was driving, Brinco liked to go slowly so he could enjoy the sight of the wall with the company's name and emblem. A swordfish and narwhal. Underneath were the inter-twined initials 'B&L Frozen Foods'. This time Inverno also drove slowly, but Brinco's attention was centred on the yard in front of the warehouse, which was devoid of vehicles. They must have left, he thought. The old woman can't have realised they've gone back.

Víctor got out of the jeep and jangled the keys like a rattle. Suddenly he stopped playing around and stared at Inverno. 'The dogs? Why aren't the dogs barking?'

They left them loose inside the warehouse. They'd always bark excitedly and whine behind the doors. They recognised the sound of the Land Rover's engine from afar.

He whistled. Called out to them: 'Sil! Neil!'

This was the involuntary signal. The doors opened and out walked two stocky men holding cocked pistols equipped with silencers. Inverno had held back. As a precaution. He'd also grabbed hold of his weapon. But from the right of the warehouse, from behind a fuel tank, came another guy, aiming a sawn-off shotgun.

They were skilled and highly trained. An office job to get back the two-thirds that was owing.

Brinco had miscalculated the payment period. He'd thought he had more time. But just as he was sending a message, the office had taken the initiative.

They pushed them inside. The guy with the shotgun stayed downstairs in the warehouse, aiming at Inverno after tying him up. The two dogs, a German shepherd and a Dobermann, lay dead. Little blood for so much silence.

The other two went upstairs with Brinco, one behind and the other in front. He dialled the number he was told to.

'Hello? Milton here.'

The person talking deliberately emphasised his name. He didn't want the other man blurting out his real name. The one buzzing about inside Víctor Rumbo's head.

'Milton, this is no way to behave.'

223

One of his assailants, standing behind him, suddenly began to strangle him with a kind of thin wire. He felt the wire penetrating his skin. Making a furrow. Feeling the pain, he instinctively tried to resist. He banged with his elbows, gasping for breath, but the assailant opposite him stuck the barrel of his gun against Brinco's forehead. The other loosened the wire. And the one with the gun told him to pick up the receiver again.

'Ah, music, sweet music. Compliments of the house. The best material for tuning. They're doing their job. They're professionals. You're a professional. That's how it's done.'

Brinco passed his free hand over his neck. The sensation that an invisible cord was still pressing into it. The digital stain of blood.

'Listen, Milton. We had a problem with a partner. The guy who was supposed to make the payment was trustworthy. This has never happened before. He lost his head.'

'Yes, yes, of course. That's what they've been complaining about. They don't want it happening again. We deal with serious people, not kids.'

'He lost control of the situation. Hanged himself yesterday. You can check this out if you like.'

'Don't come to me with videos. It's a very sad story. Don't air it any more. Cover up the hole and leave it. You can do that now, can't you?'

'Yes, of course I can . . . He hanged himself, that's all. I think it was my fault. I pushed him too far . . .'

'The world is a valley of tears. Why walk about with a tombstone around your neck? I'm going to hang up. This is a public phone. Grow up a bit!'

Brinco glanced at the wall clock.

'You're right, Milton. There's no point drowning in a cup of water. I'll give these gentlemen the treatment they deserve.'

He hung up. Passed his hand over his neck again. Took a deep breath.

'Good, let's see to that debt, shall we, piano tuner? You killed the dogs now, didn't you? Well, right underneath the doghouse is the bag with the money.'

They left the office. The warehouse was empty. The automatic shutters started to rise. Neither henchman had time to ask what was going on. Chumbo, Inverno and half a dozen armed men overpowered them.

'Where's the other guy?' asked Brinco.

'In the fridge, taking some fresh air,' said Inverno, pointing to one of the cold storage rooms.

Brinco rummaged in his assailant's pocket. Found what he was looking for. Tautened the piano string.

'You know? I just felt a strange pleasure, something I'd never felt before.'

Milton decided to place the call reserved for extreme circumstances.

If happiness is to travel from cold to hot, he'd gone in the opposite direction. From a hot sweat, the atmosphere of a large hotel's kitchen and the euphoria of someone who has the power of intimidation and uses it, to the cold sweat of someone whose internal affairs have been badly disturbed. As a boy he'd lived in Moravia, in a settlement raised on a mountain of rubbish. He'd grown on top of the discarded waste of Medellín's rich quarters. There the floor of his home gave off a sticky smell through the cracks, the methane that emanates from decomposition. The senses learn. They reject the base smell in order to perceive the rest. But the day comes when the methane sweeps away all the laboriously constructed scents. And the settlement burns. Moravia burns.

Which is why he always took quick decisions, a 'Do it!' whenever he got a whiff of methane. As now. There was a telephone in the kitchen, which he'd been watching for hours. He decided to take every precaution. He removed his head chef's uniform, put on a holster and jacket. Loaded the magazine in his automatic.

'I'll be back in a minute. Pay attention to the phone. Don't go to sleep on me.'

He made the call from a public booth in a small square next to the Hotel Coruña Road. He had no idea who Palindrome was, but he knew it would work. Palindrome answered. Yes, sir. Milton here. From Madrid, that's right. It was an emergency. He'd lost track of some men he'd sent to Galicia. They were his best archangels, though he didn't say this. They'd gone to collect a debt. An office job. They were supposed to call. In a maximum of twelve hours. But he hadn't heard from them for a day and a half. The debtor? Brinco's group. In Noitía.

There was a silence. He couldn't tell what the silence smelled of because his head was overwhelmed by methane.

'Understood. Thank you for the information. First of all, calm. And no noise.'

In the hotel lobby, a receptionist gestured with his hand, came out from behind the counter and rushed over to him. 'Boss. We got a call in reception. A strange call. They said they've left the piano at the door to the warehouse.'

'The piano?'

'That's what they said. Nothing else. A piano for Milton.'

That's right. Everything so clean. The stink of methane.

'Warn the kitchen! Tell everybody to go to the entrance to the warehouse. With their weapons!'

The warehouse was reached down an alleyway that opened out into a patio at the back of the hotel. Milton's men took up position there and at the entrance to the alley. The only thing in the way, right in the middle of the patio, was a large crate. Water poured out from between the boards. Two metres long and half a metre wide, more or less. Everything required by a man packed in ice who'd come to deliver a piano string.

Inverno communicated with Chumbo by means of a walkie-talkie. He occupied the shade next to the sea gate of Romance Manor. Sentinel for Leda and Santiago. By the shore, the water around his waist, the boy was swimming, or pretending to swim, with some goggles. Each dive was followed by a series of shouts and gestures aimed at attracting his mother's attention.

Leda watched him. Returned his attention. She was alone, sitting on a towel on the beach, wearing a printed T-shirt that seemed to attract all the breeze.

On a boat anchored next to some rocks that acted as a natural embankment, dressed in sea clothes, pretending to be a fisherman seeing to his nets, was Chumbo, holding a Winchester kept out of sight on deck.

There were two more people, hidden, but taking part in this unfolding drama. Fins and Mara on a dune, behind the marram's herbal screen. The rumours of a settling of scores in Brinco's circle had brought them here, to this oblique position as the capo's bodyguards. But the capo was nowhere to be seen.

Mara whispered ironically to Fins, 'Everybody watching the lady of the shipwrecks.'

And the lady of the shipwrecks watching everything. She was blinded for a moment by the sun glinting on the water. She set about reconstructing everything. First of all, the child. His greeting calmed her. She'd been like this for days. An activated inner sense that kept her on the alert. Permanently ill at ease. Checking out every single place, trying to turn any sound into a murmur, a source of information.

A diver emerged on the port side of the boat where Chumbo was. Chumbo had his back to him. When he turned, alerted by the splashing, the diver fired a harpoon into his chest.

Reality is an outer layer. There is a hidden world. And in this hidden world there is a conflict of forces which for her take on the shape of currents, underwater angels. For years the sea has sent her good signals. Even at the time of the accident, when the explosion sank Lucho Malpica's boat, her father was saved. He almost couldn't swim. The current took him in its arms, after he'd chafed himself against rock after rock, and deposited him on the beach.

Leda got up in a state of agitation. Surveyed the blanket of water, the glittering crumbs, that infinite, ephemeral silverwork a hand of wind had wrought on the sunny sea. She suddenly felt this was a place of horror. She couldn't shout. She ran and could hear – a sticky, faulty sound – the whistle of her own drowning.

Santiago finally reappeared. Took off his goggles and waved at his mother.

'How long can you stay under without breathing?'

'You what?'

'How long can you stay under without breathing?'

Leda heard a violent roar. She quickly identified where it was. It was coming from the palafittic horizon of the mussel rafts. It was a speedboat heading quickly towards the beach. Inverno came out of his lookout post by the sea gate of Romance Manor. Tried to speak to Chumbo, but got no answer. All he could hear was the sea moaning. The strangest thing was that Chumbo was there, on his boat. Inverno could perceive his silhouette in the distance. He had his back to him. Must have been trying to work out the nature of this piercing sound approaching over the sea.

He decided to expose himself and head for Leda and the child while trying to establish communication with Chumbo.

'Chumbo, can you hear me? Over.'

The sound of interference like a hum.

Something burning tore into his shoulder. Another bullet smashed his head open.

How could Chumbo possibly kill Inverno? Even for something like that, he'd have asked for permission.

But there he was, firing a rifle from the deck. That blasted Judas.

Instead of taking to her heels, Leda did something surprising. She took Inverno's weapon, protected the child behind her and aimed at the place of betrayal. Let him see what rotten wood he was really made of.

'Chumbo, you son of a bitch!'

But the marksman responded by carefully aiming his precision rifle. Leda realised her reaction was absurd and they had no way out. Chumbo was part of the enemy. The marksman wasn't going to stop the speedboat roaring towards them.

She grabbed Santiago by the arm and they ran barefoot across the sand. The sand that loved her so much now seemed to restrain their feet. When the child fell on his knees and she tried to pull him up, to Leda's disbelief, help came from the hidden world.

'Lie down beside him and don't move!' shouted Fins.

They waited for the speedboat to come alongside the shore. There were three crewmen. Two of them got ready to jump while the third kept the speedboat steady.

'They're not out to kill them, they're out to kidnap them!' exclaimed Mara.

It was time to shoot. And for the sea to lend a miraculous hand. For the reports to multiply several times over. As sometimes happens.

43

The tolling of the bells has to make itself heard above the seagulls' chatter, their scandalmongering on top of St Mary's cemetery in Noitía.

'They're always after people, keeping an eye out, throwing insults.'

The old sailor glances at the sky in disapproval. He is one of the few not wearing a tie, the same as his companion. The top button of his shirt squeezes his Adam's apple. As he lifts his head, the white points of the collar grow tense. They're dressed very similarly, in black suits and waistcoats, but the top button makes a difference. His companion's collar is open. There's also a contrast in the whiteness and style of their hair. His hair forms a crest ending in a summit, a kind of wick on top of his forehead. His face is heavily lined, but his seniority is somehow intemporal, as if he's returned from another age. His partner's hair has been carefully combed, a humid whiteness, possibly smarmed down in such a way as to conceal any bald patches. They're both tall and upright for their years. The main difference is in the way they walk. The position of their arms. One seems to be carrying a weight. A sack. A body. His own. Without the use of hands.

'Crows have a bad reputation, Edmundo, but theirs is a different way of knowing.'

'Talking of birds, there was a guy in Veracruz who kept trying to tell me, "You sure know a lot about tweety birds!"'

They walk slowly, at low tide, paying careful attention to the movements of the cars, mostly high-cylinder, bringing people to the ceremony.

'Look at that, Companion! Never mind the width, feel the quality,' mutters Edmundo, the sailor who played Christ on the day of the Passion.

'The bigger the better!' replies Lucho.

When they reach the niches, they move apart from the rest of the gathering.

'This is one of the healthiest places in the world! That's why I came back,' says Edmundo. 'The niche was fully paid for.'

'It's certainly sunny.'

'Great views, too.' Edmundo wishes to encourage the Companion as best he can. He gestures towards the cemetery in contrast with the new urban buildings of irregular, exaggerated heights. 'And just look at the skyline!'

And then in the Companion's ear, 'They haven't had to sleep out before.'

'They certainly lived the way they wanted to. At a hundred miles per hour.'

'Or more!'

The two coffins are almost entirely obscured by ribboned wreaths. The Requiem Mass is led by the parish priest in a surplice and black stole, assisted by two other priests. 'Eternal rest grant unto them, O Lord, and let perpetual light shine upon them . . . And upon the rest of us so that no other curse like this descends upon Noitía.'

The people cluster around the priests in an atmosphere of commotion. Together with painful, tearful expressions, there are others marked by tense vigilance. At the axis of the ceremony, on the other side of the priest, is Mariscal, guarded by the impassive Carburo.

'As it says in the *Miserere mei, Deus*, David's penitential psalm, "Have mercy upon me, O God, wash me thoroughly from my wickedness . . . Thou shalt wash me, and I shall be whiter than snow."'

As he speaks, he tries not to look at anybody. This is his habit. But today is starting to be a strange day for him. He's receiving signals about a war he would have preferred to ignore. For a moment he notices Santiago, the boy with the patch, staring at him with a single eye. A panoptic eye. An eye that sees everything. Records everything. He observes Leda, the mother, curling a strand of the boy's hair in her fingers. On the other side is Sira. Ever since the incident on Romance beach, considered a kidnap attempt, the mother and boy have been living in the fortress of the Ultramar. He's heard the odd rumour that Mariscal has been studying Leda's anatomy there. For goodness' sake! The ears are for hearing. He knows full well they're father and daughter.

He wrote what he has to say the previous evening. He thought about it word for word. But now he's unsure about the script. He also received a visit from Brinco last night. He's sorry he couldn't say no to this ridiculous idea of his. He's ashamed to think that his faint-hearted attitude, his yieldingness, may have had a causal relationship with the payment for the funeral and the generous donation Brinco made on the spot. As he is looking around, he comes across another panoptic being, the impression of a single eye with dark glasses behind the image of a marble archangel on top of a sarcophagus. Another old acquaintance, Fins Malpica, attending the farewell ritual. He recalls what he said at his father's funeral, 'The sea prefers the brave ones.' He was sorry about that death. He wasn't a believer, he'd said to Lucho, but he'd make a first-rate Christ. And when Lucho died as a result of the dynamite, he found it impossible to ask any questions. He blamed the sea. With a favourable report he helped the boy attend a school for orphans. And receive a grant for university. He also lent a hand so he'd be accepted in the police academy. Fins never attended Mass. Just once, recently, he'd come to see the priest. Behaved impertinently. Asked who the mausoleum was for.

'What mausoleum? It's a pantheon.'

'A bit bigger than the rest, isn't it? So who's it for?'

'Why are you asking if you already know? Doesn't the Brancana family have the right to a pantheon?'

'A palace, you mean,' Fins had replied. 'A monument to dirty money. You should know how such filth is viewed in the beyond, but the way I see it, everything started quite differently, with a manger in Bethlehem.'

Here the priest had cut him short. Nobody had the right to lecture him on doctrine. 'When you've finished, you know where the door is.'

'Real judgement is not that meted out by men on earth. So it will be for our neighbours and brothers in faith, Fernando Inverno and Carlos Chumbo. They will have to appear before true justice. At the Last Judgement St Michael's scales will weigh the value of souls for God. And then we will find out how much their souls weighed. All we know is that they were generous to those around them and to the Church of God.'

The priest glances over at the temple and nods to a parishioner standing at the bottom of the bell tower.

'Every year Inverno and Chumbo made their donations to Our Lady of the Sea, the Virgin of Mount Carmel. It was Inverno who paid for the new bells. So it's only right they should ring at his funeral.'

The bells begin to toll. Fins enjoys the sound. He thinks the historical prestige of bells is due to the fact that they don't lie. There's another sound that doesn't lie in Noitía. That of the cow by the lighthouse which moos whenever the mist is so thick it swallows up the light of the beacon.

In his position, half concealed by the angel, Fins removes his dark glasses. And looks at Leda. She imitates his gesture. Slowly takes off her glasses. Closes and opens her eyes in a blink that seems timed to the bells.

The priest continues the funeral oration with an air of apparent routine:

'"I am the resurrection and the life. He that believeth in me, though he were dead, yet shall he live. And whosoever liveth and believeth in me shall never die." God is light, he sees everything, hears everything. Knows everything. What's going on in the darkest corner. In the grottos of the sea and the depths of the soul. Our faith may stumble. We may ask where God is, why he remains in silence.'

Don Marcelo's voice suddenly begins to shake. He seems bewildered, overcome by the turn of events. Gives the impression he is not going to be able to advance beyond that full stop, that 'silence'. But suddenly he is transfigured. He's not praying any more, he's shouting:

'God isn't stupid! He hasn't come to pussyfoot around. As the psalmist says:

'He smote the first-born of Egypt,
both of man and beast.
He hath sent tokens and wonders into the midst of thee,
    O thou land of Egypt,
upon Pharaoh and all his servants.'

The psalm is like a deposit of wind and gives his voice an unusual preponderance:

> 'As for the images of the heathen, they are but silver
>   and gold,
> the work of men's hands.
> They have mouths, and speak not.
> They have eyes, and see not.
> They have ears, and hear not.
> Neither is there any breath in their mouths.'

He pauses. This hasn't happened to him for quite some time, being able to hear and understand his own words.

'Thus the Lord speaks. He gives us breath and takes it away again. May they rest in peace.'

The workmen place the coffins inside their niches. This is followed by the sound of banging tools. A hammer nailing in wooden covers. The gravestone being slid into place. The final rubric. The priest quickly greets several family members. Offers a sentence of consolation that is left hanging in the air. Then turns to address Mariscal. 'The religious ceremony has finished. It's up to you what you do now.'

'Thank you, Marcelo. You know that's my favourite psalm. Shame not to hear it in Latin!'

'Víctor came to see me,' says the priest, cutting him off. 'I don't like the entertainment he's prepared. This is sacred ground.'

'It's a tribute to both of them. Inverno played music all his life. He had the mark of the trumpet on his lips. There were even concerts where they rode on horseback. Noitía's Magicians was their name.'

'In Noitía a funeral was always a funeral, and a party a party.'

'Patience, Marcelo. Remember the first-born of Egypt are in charge!'

'I'm going. My work here is done.'

'Thank God your work is never done, Marcelo. You have to take care of us, your flock. *Agnus Dei, qui tollis peccata mundi, miserere nobis.* We must meet some day and have a chat about Unamuno.'

As the priest leaves, from the far side of the cemetery, hidden until that moment, emerge the members of a mariachi quartet. The musicians, dressed in typical Mexican clothes, perform the ballad 'Pero sigo siendo el rey'.

A murmur of surprise ripples around the cemetery. Followed by several disapproving looks. This has never happened before in Noitía. The most there was, and this was some time ago, was a bagpipe intoning a solemn march. But as the ballad progresses, the faces take on a renewed sort of expression.

'If the acoustics are good,' says Edmundo, 'in three minutes you'll have yourself an age-old tradition.'

'That's the thing about death,' replies the Companion. 'It lends itself to everything.'

44

It was a refreshing sensation to be in one of the miradors used by Mariscal and not to have to hide, stay under cover, but instead to share the view. What was happening was more than unusual. It struck him as nothing short of miraculous. Because of the person by his side and the topic of conversation. Grimaldo had bumped into him in the station car park. Fins had expected a peevish greeting. Or nothing at all. But in the end he'd spat out a kind of telegram: 'Meet me at the mirador in Corveiro. In fifteen minutes.'

'I know you don't trust me,' he said when they were there. 'You do well. Never trust me. But today make an exception.'

Haroldo Micho Grimaldo had the appearance of a dandy from the suburbs, just like the Old Man. A single policeman, he was the only guest in a boarding house whose mistress treated him like a king, viewing any other candidate as a small-time crook who'd come to the wrong door. He didn't have a shining reputation, at the police station anyway. Though paradoxically he was, or proclaimed himself to be, the Scourge of Vice. One of his roles was to inspect so-called singles clubs, a euphemism he took it upon himself to clarify.

'Singles clubs? Whorehouses, you mean.'

Proceedings were sometimes begun, but none of the

brothels was ever closed. Except when there was a scandal, an argument leading to injuries or casualties, which transcended the barrier of night. This control was vital in the fight against prostitution rings. So Micho Grimaldo was a cynic. Or more than that. Most people thought more than that. This being the case, the strangest thing about his behaviour was that he wasn't more hypocritical when it came to his impression of an exemplary life. There were periods when he did his best. His virtuous days, as he liked to call them. When his tongue became sharper than usual, like a cut-throat razor. But after that he'd let himself go. Roll from club to club with the repellent air of a perfumer. If others put up with him, it was because he was on the verge of retiring. And because he knew a lot. Or so people supposed. In the past he'd worked for the Political-Social Brigade, whose job it was to hunt down opponents of Franco's regime. He'd been involved in Barcelona and Madrid. And then returned to his birthplace. He'd inherited a country house from his father, all refurbished, in a village inland, but hardly ever went there. He'd acquired an exciting new identity in his role against vice. Being a whoremonger.

'Well, are you going to trust me or not? I can't bear know-it-all silences.'

'Go ahead, Grimaldo,' said Fins.

It was dusk. The estuary was like a log, burning from the inside out. Behind them, the darkness slipped whistling over the eucalyptus leaves.

Micho Grimaldo took a stick and began to draw a map on the ground. The axis was the river Miño. He traced the iron bridge at Tui. Despite the conditions, he exhibited a wish for accuracy. He marked the main towns on either side of the border with dots and joined them up with lines representing roads.

'This Sunday there's going to be a party,' he said. 'An important party. With the excuse of a wedding. Not many guests, very select ones. The party's going to be here, in the Lower Miño, in a place named Quinta da Velha Saudade. Not far away is an old quarry. There is a track, about a hundred yards long, with a turn-off leading to a site for abandoned machinery. A good spot to hide your car. You'll have to climb a bit, then go through a forest which runs parallel to the road. On the other side of the road, after a bend, is the mansion. A large terrace overlooking the estuary. High walls. Two entrances. But cars can only go in and out through an automatic gate. When they leave, they have to observe a stop sign, which is right on the bend.'

He'd leaned down in order to draw on the ground and straightened up slowly, holding on to his hips. He stared at Fins. 'You have to be there! On the sly, of course. Take note of everything on your camera. And that's all I'm going to say.'

'Are you going as well?'

'Didn't I tell you it was an important party?' he scoffed.

The man was fat – 'adipose', Mara Doval would have said – but seemed to have been whittled down by the shade. He erased the map with his shoes. Then sought out the final embers of the setting sun on the sea.

'I received two medical reports today. One bad: I have cancer. The other good: it's progressing rapidly.'

He opened the door of his Dodge. Before leaving, he turned to Fins and remarked with an air of distance, 'Don't mistake confidence for compassion. If I'm telling you this, it's not because of my soul. It's because of you. Because I understand you haven't sold yourself. Yet.'

He emerged slowly on to the road, let the car descend the

hill in neutral. It was a long time before he switched on the lights.

From his hiding place, Fins had photographed all the cars leaving Quinta da Velha Saudade. With his zoom he'd managed to make out Montiglio. Then Mariscal with Carburo driving. After an interval in which the occupants of the cars had been strangers, mostly young, with a festive air, probably no more than guests, he'd focused on another familiar vehicle. The Alfa Romeo in which the lawyer Óscar Mendoza was travelling on his own. He'd seemed to wait far too long at the stop sign, even though there weren't any other cars on the road. But finally he'd pulled off in the direction of the border.

The sun was about to go down. It didn't bother his eyes any more. On the contrary, this emigrant beauty struck him as the best gift of the day.

Fins glanced at his watch. Thought about leaving, but something held him back. It wasn't to do with the outside, but with his own mind, which had been influenced by the long wait in front of a gate that kept opening and closing. What was going on inside his mind wasn't an absence on account of the *petit mal*, but the memory of an absence. What happened when an absence took place. Those moments of timelessness which were, however, extremely brief. He could see Leda with a serious expression, measuring time on the stopwatch of her fingers. This image merged with the first time he remembered seeing her. Of course he'd seen her before, when she was a girl, but this was the first time his eyes had focused on her presence to the exclusion of everything else, the day she painted her nails. She'd found a bottle in the sand, that way she had of walking as if excavating the ground. The container was small, conical, made of thick glass.

In the palm of her hand, despite the coating of sand, her discovery had an animal appearance, a kind of alert immobility, a red ampoule which grew when she wet it and rubbed it with her thumb. That was when she placed her right foot on a rock, among limpets. Her foot was no longer a girl's. It must have grown overnight. She opened the bottle brought by the sea and, using the brush in the lid, slowly painted her toenails.

'It was eight seconds, Mrs Malpica,' said Leda with reference to the absence.

Now she thought about it, the mother's strange reticence, irrational anger whenever the girl turned up, may have had to do with the information in her hands. The fact that she was in on the secret. The intimacy of measuring the length of each absence.

'Forget about it, girl,' she said to Leda one day after Leda had told her about the absence he'd had in the School of Indians. 'I don't want everyone talking about it.'

Leda answered with that manner she had from another time: 'For me it will be as if a stone fell into a well.'

The iron gate opened again, activated from the inside. Out came a car he failed to recognise. A surprising automobile that put all his motoring knowledge to the test. A very special BMW. He realised Delmiro Oliveira had a passion for the classics. From time to time he'd appeared in a Ford Falcon or an imposing Chrysler Imperial with whitewall tyres. Like the others, he was forced to stop in order to join the main road.

Fins focused on the driver. On Don Delmiro. Then on the passenger in dark glasses. He didn't allow any idea, any emotion, to reach his finger. He clicked his camera. That's right. In his imagination the enlarger was already projecting the image on Baryta paper. A work of art that would go down in history.

Next to Delmiro Oliveira, on board a BMW 501, a Barockengel, he had just photographed the Baroque Angel of motoring, Lieutenant Colonel Humberto Alisal.

A car on the road had been in an accident. And burned. A Portuguese National Republican Guard stood with an extinguisher, contemplating the heavy, bewildered billowing of smoke sedated by foam around the accident. The guard turned and gestured to Fins to carry on driving. What made him hold back was the sight of the blanket on the side of the road. He pulled over and went to have a look. A second guard, near the body, was writing something in a notebook that was too small for his hands and pen. Fins didn't have to remove the blanket. The lawyer Óscar Mendoza's head, with wide-open eyes, seemed to want to detach itself from the rest of his body. It hadn't burned. The impact must have been so strong it flung him straight out through the windscreen. The blood from the wounds on his face had acquired the density of flies. Fins glanced at the tarmac. Couldn't make out any skid marks. He considered the barest gesture of covering Mendoza's face, but ignored his conscience and thought about his camera. The car. Getting away.

'Did you know this man?'

'No, I've never seen him before.'

'Then, please, take your car out of here and let us get on with our work.'

45

Cons lighthouse cast its first circular beam over Noitía and the lights went on like candles in a line. The same beam passed its hand over the whitewall tyres of Mariscal's Mercedes-Benz in the deserted mirador. The Old Man soon felt a second beam on his back, a noisy, piercing shaft. He knew who this was. He could paint a portrait of people by the way they drove.

Brinco's was a face of impatient greed. Greed was OK. But not impatience. Job's patience had been rewarded. It was a shame people didn't read the Old Testament. Jehovah had given Job twice as much as he'd had before. Fourteen thousand sheep, six thousand camels, a thousand yoke of oxen and a thousand donkeys.

He couldn't fail to recognise the pilot by the way he braked and slammed the door. The noise disrupted his vision of the final red glow as the sun sank into the outer sea.

'How was the funeral?' asked Brinco.

'I've seen better ones. The priest and the mariachis weren't bad.'

Mariscal walked to the edge of the cliff and, without turning around, said, 'Someone ran over Dead Man's Hand's wife this morning. The driver took off. They obviously meant to kill him. But the wife got in the way. Fell down dead on top of him.'

'Poor woman, going before him!'

Mariscal ignored his comment. 'More people are dying than we can cope with.'

'Perhaps I should disappear for a while.'

He was relieved to hear this declaration. Stroked the small Astra .38 special on his chest to put it to sleep. Then turned around. 'Go far away, son.'

'Where to? The inferno?'

'A little further, if you can.'

The light of the moon illuminated part of the map on the floor of the School of Indians. The rest was aged darkness. Leda and Fins inhabited the edge of the chiaroscuro.

'Why didn't you go with him? You should get out of here with your son. Anything could happen.'

'He didn't ask me.'

'He'll be arriving in Río about now. We're going to keep track of him. I can pass you information. Just for you.'

Leda ignored his proposal. She was sure Brinco hadn't boarded that flight from Porto. He'd have sent someone else in his place. Or vanished on the steps of the plane, in an airport worker's luminous jacket. He'd done this before. She was the one who'd arranged to meet Fins in the School of Indians. She wanted to see if the bait on the hook worked. She didn't regret it. It was a fitting tribute. To the bait.

She asked, 'Is it true you know how to touch-type?'

'What does that matter now?'

'Sit down then! I want you to write a letter for me. You know I never got a letter?'

'I don't have any paper.'

'It doesn't matter. Type anyway. I like to hear the singing

245

of the bars. I'll dictate . . . "Dear friend, now that all is mute silense . . ." Did you write "silense" with an "s"?'

'Yes.'

'Good.'

Leda found it difficult to carry on the game. The spines of words in her throat. 'How was it? "Now that all is loneliness, pain . . ." No, better not write that.'

Fins took his hands off the keyboard. 'I wasn't going to anyway.'

The roof groaned with the tragedy of night. Someone poured liquid through the skylight and threw in a lit piece of cloth.

But there wasn't just fire.

The sound of a shot pinged off the typewriter. Fins flung himself to the ground, drew his revolver and instinctively sought shelter beneath the Underwood's tiny shield.

'Go where it's dark!' he shouted to Leda.

From the fire, the intruder shot at the darkness, but soon turned his attention back to the figure huddled beneath the teacher's desk. A shot hit Fins' shoulder. It was obvious, the intruder must have known, because Fins' face was exposed, contorted with pain, in the moonlight, at the feet of the blind mannequin and the one-armed skeleton. But the intruder was also exposed, the length of his body, as he proudly grasped the powerful shape of a Star. Never trust an automatic. The ocean around the equator caught fire. Fins shot his revolver and the shadow fell like a sack of sand on top of the flames. A thick smoke, as from a volcano, crept all over the map.

'Where are you, Leda?'

He shouted several times. Got no answer. Dragged himself outside, convinced he'd find her there.

* * *

Carburo stood in the doorway of the Ultramar, watching the fire on the hill. 'Boss, boss! The old school is burning!'

Mariscal shoved him aside. Took a few steps forward, leaning on his staff.

'It's burning again, boss!'

He grumbled without turning around, 'I can see that. I can see it's burning.'

He started walking towards the fire. Accompanied by a small crowd.

His eyes were wide open. Seemed to be gazing at the trickle of blood. Brinco lay dead in the ocean. After the initial blaze this was a meek fire, trying to gnaw at the noble wood. Where it grew was over in the darkness, where the pupils' desks had been stacked up. From there the flames aimed for the roof. The smoke disorientated the bats, which flew into the walls and from time to time collided with the mannequin and the skeleton. Had they been able to see, Brinco's eyes would have met Leda's. She was a little further south. Near Cape Verde. From there, down towards the Antarctic, a part of the map had been disjointed. Leda lifted the plank, using an iron bar, and revealed a leather suitcase lying on the seabed. Full of wads of notes, except for a gap in the middle with pharmaceutical tools. An Astra Llama pistol. Chelín's pendulum.

With Carburo for company, Mariscal approached the outside of the school, where people were assembling.

'Shall we put out the fire, Mariscal?' asked a voice.

He swung around in a rage. Glared at them all. The shadow of the flames reflected on their faces. Glinting in their eyes as they climbed the back of night. An ancient mirror whose mercury was pouring out. A hypnotic silence whose only sound was the scoffing of flames. He thought they all owed him something. Would do whatever he commanded. But he was overcome by an unusual feeling, something he'd never experienced before. The fear of his own kind.

'What are you asking me for?'

The other person didn't know what to say. Felt confused by the Old Man's reaction. The anger in his voice. Especially when the Old Man added, 'Who am I, after all?'

He scrutinised every face. Conducted an inspection. They glanced at each other enquiringly. Things to do with the Old Man. Everybody remained quiet. The only sound the flames gnawing at the cracks, the umbilical resistance of ivy and stone.

Leda emerged from the school barefoot, her feet, arms and face blackened. At a gesture from Mariscal, Carburo went over to her and took the suitcase. Someone finally paid attention to Fins, who was leaning against the wall, badly wounded, squeezing his shoulder to stem the flow of blood. Leda glanced at him as she passed. Just for a moment. The length of an absence.

'Is there anybody else left inside?' Mariscal asked her.

'No.'

Mariscal cleared a way through the barrier of people. Seemed to have difficulty walking, leaning on his cane, but only to start with. As Leda approached, he passed his hand over her blackened cheek, with the care of a portrait artist, and then put his arms around her.

'Come on, girl, let's go.'

Carburo followed behind, with the suitcase. Mariscal glanced over at the veteran porter.

'What have we here?'

'Oh, nothing,' replied Leda. 'Things of mine. Memories mostly.'

And Mariscal murmured:

'Memories, eh? Then it must be heavy.'

www.vintage-books.co.uk